# The

# Gnostic

# Mystery

# The Gnostic Mystery

by
Randy Davila

Hierophant

The Gnostic Mystery
By Randy Davila

Published by:
Hierophant Publishing
8301 Broadway, Suite 219
San Antonio, TX 78209
(210) 829-0570
www.hierophantpublishing.com

Quote by Anthony de Mello, SJ, from the Doubleday edition of *The Heart of the Enlightened*.

LCCN: 2008932970

**Publisher's Cataloging-in-Publication**
(Provided by Quality Books, Inc.)


Davila, Randy.
  The gnostic mystery / by Randy Davila.
  p. cm.
  Includes bibliographical references.
  ISBN-13: 978-0-9818771-0-5
    ISBN-10: 0-9818771-0-9


    1. Gnosticism--Fiction.  2. Christianity--Fiction.
  3. Jerusalem--Fiction.  4. Historical fiction.
  I. Title.

    PS3604.A9545G56 2008        813'.6
                    QBI08-600199

Hier⊕phant
Publishing

For Mia

*Special thanks to ET, TF, AE, PG, and ES, whose work and support were instrumental in the creation of this novel.*

The devotee knelt to be initiated into discipleship. The guru whispered the sacred mantra into his ear, warning him not to reveal it to anyone.

"What will happen if I do?" asked the initiate.

Said the guru, "Anyone to whom you reveal the mantra will be liberated from ignorance and suffering, but you yourself will be excluded from discipleship and suffer damnation."

No sooner had he heard these words than the initiate rushed to the marketplace, collected a large crowd around him, and repeated the sacred mantra for all to hear.

The other disciples reported this to the guru and demanded that the man be expelled from the monastery for his disobedience.

The guru smiled and said, "He has no need of anything I can teach. His action has shown him to be a guru in his own right."

– Anthony de Mello, SJ

I

The Philosophy and Religion Department was tucked deep inside the University of Jerusalem's West Complex. Jack and Punjeeh navigated the building's maze of intersecting hallways in search of Chloe's office, Jack's anticipation growing with every step. He was anxious to read the translation of the ancient scroll he acquired a day earlier, but he was also excited to see Chloe again.

Jack had been trying to get more information about her from Punjeeh all morning, but this was one area in which his friend wasn't very talkative.

"She's a nice lady," Punjeeh said. "She grew up in Greece and moved here to take a professorship at the college two years ago. I understand she is very popular with the students, as Esther says her classes fill quite quickly ... there's not much more to tell, really."

"So what's the story with this Ben fellow?" Jack pressed.

Punjeeh looked momentarily puzzled and then chuckled aloud. "Ben? Oh ... well, I think you'll have to ask her about that one," he said coyly.

They arrived at Chloe's office and found her seated behind a mahogany desk in a brown leather high-back office chair. The office itself looked like a well-kept mini-library: Bookshelves climbed all four walls, each stuffed with texts of varying shapes and sizes. Chloe was talking with a distinguished-looking, balding gentleman in his mid-fifties. Jack immediately noticed the scroll, which was unrolled in the center of her desk.

"Knock, knock," Punjeeh said as they peered through the open doorway.

"Please come in." Chloe stood and motioned them forward. The older gentlemen also stood to face them. Once erect, his tall, thin frame became more pronounced, towering over the rest of the group.

"This is Professor King," Chloe said, "our department chairperson and resident expert on Christianity. He's an ordained minister in the Anglican Church and has a PhD in early church history."

Jack and Punjeeh introduced themselves and exchanged handshakes with Professor King.

"Quite a find you have here, gentlemen," Professor King said in a deep voice that betrayed a hint of an Oxford accent.

"Don't look at me," Punjeeh said. "This one belongs to Jack."

"Thank you," Jack replied enthusiastically. "Everyone gets lucky once in a while." He looked over at Chloe. "So what exactly have we got here, anyway?"

"The answer is complicated," she acknowledged. "Please, sit down."

Professor King resumed his seat while Jack and Punjeeh took the chairs next to him. They leaned over the desk and examined the scroll. Now that they were closer, Jack noticed a plain piece of white paper with a handwritten paragraph in English on the desk next to the scroll, which he assumed was the translation.

He could also see Chloe better. She looked even more attractive than in their first meeting the night before. She wore a black suit-skirt that came to her knees, a red blouse the color of her lipstick, and her jet black hair was pulled back in a bun, which contrasted well with her amber-green eyes. Her wire-frame glasses offered the only hint of her profession, and they sat neatly on her cute pug nose.

"I think the easiest thing to do is have you read my translation," Chloe began, waking Jack from his daydream, "and then hopefully Professor King and I can help you make some sense of it."

Chloe turned the piece of paper around and slid it across the desk. Jack could feel his heart beating faster as he read the following:

*Oh Valentinus and Basilides, if only you were here to see what has come to pass.*

*What we started, they have overtaken.*

*The emperor claims a great vision of our Risen Lord and has become one of them. Oh what deception! If they only knew of Mithras, Dionysus, Osiris, and the many, many more.*

*His gathering at Nicea has decreed their ignorance. The Emperor's mother has descended upon Jerusalem and spread falsehoods. The unification of church and state is complete.*

*In Rome, our brothers and sisters in Gnosis are being murdered. Our writings are called heretical and thrown into the fire.*

*Forgive them Lord, for they know not what they do.*

*But what shall become of the Secret Mysteries? Shall they die with me? They must not. I will record the First Secret Mystery of Jesus and hide it within the caves of our forefathers. Let God keep it safe from destruction, and ordain whoever finds it, so that the truth and the mystery shall someday be reborn.*

Chloe and Professor King sat silently as Jack and Punjeeh read and reread the translation. Finally, Punjeeh spoke. "This is fascinating. When do you think it was written?"

"If it's authentic," said Professor King, raising a finger, "and at first glance I have no reason to believe that it's not, I would place it sometime in the mid-fourth century. Definitely after 325 AD, when the Council of Nicaea took place."

Again Jack found himself on unfamiliar ground. In his other life back in the United States, he was the expert in most situations. At work, people came to him with questions, but here he was the one asking all of them. "The council of what?"

"Nicaea," answered Professor King. "It was a meeting of Literalist Christian bishops and a precursor to the formation of the Roman Catholic Church. This document appears to be written by a Gnostic Christian who was dissatisfied with the union of the Catholic Church and the Roman Empire."

Jack's bewildered expression remained. Chloe sensed his distress and offered her assistance. "Professor, if I may?"

"By all means, Chloe, please."

"Let's look at it line by line," she began. "Some items are easier to discern than others. First, by the tone and organization, it appears that this is a letter."

Jack nodded in agreement. "To these Valentine and Basil persons."

"Right," said Chloe. "Valentinus and Basilides were very influential Gnostic teachers who lived during the second century, around 120-180 AD."

Perplexed, Punjeeh's eyes widened. "But Professor King just said this was written in the fourth century, or more than 200 years later."

"Very astute, Dr. Punjeeh," interrupted Professor King, "very astute."

Chloe smiled. "That's why I said it appears to be a letter, but in reality, I think it's more of a lamenting. The author was obviously a Gnostic Christian as evidenced by the addressing of Valentinus and Basilides in the beginning and the later line that states *our brothers and sisters in Gnosis*. But I don't think this is a letter he expected anyone to read anytime soon … so in a way, I think he was writing his epitaph."

"And in hindsight, quite possibly the epitaph of the Gnostic movement as a whole," added Professor King. "Because within a few years of this letter, the Catholic Church had consolidated its power, tortured and killed its Gnostic opponents, and destroyed virtually all the Gnostics' writings. Quite simply, the Catholic hierarchy did everything they could to permanently erase Gnostic ideology from the historical record."

# 2

*2 Days Earlier – West Bank, Israeli-occupied Palestinian territory*

"**A**re you scared?" Caleb asked.

"Of course not," Youseff scoffed as he cautiously peered down the small hole into the cavern below.

That was lie number one.

"You look scared," Caleb continued, prodding him on.

"Don't be ridiculous. What's there to be afraid of?" Youseff shot back. "It's just a cave. I've been in plenty of caves."

That was lie number two.

Youseff Muhammad and Caleb Hamad, both thirteen, were about to set the ball in motion to reveal one of the best-kept secrets of all time – but that was the furthest thing from their minds. They were simply treasure-hunting. And although finding buried treasure is a universal dream of adolescent boys, it was especially true in the small Palestinian villages around the Dead Sea, where archaeological digs were a regular occurrence and the prospects of finding something of value did not seem so remote. In a war-torn country where the poorest workers survive on less than three dollars per day, finding the right artifact could be the ticket to a new and better life.

"Throw me the rope," Youseff commanded, trying to sound confident, if only for his own benefit. Tall and stocky for his age, he regularly talked tough to impress his way upon the other boys in their village. But this type of behavior never worked on his best friend, Caleb, who, although smaller in stature, knew Youseff for what he was, a pussycat.

Caleb smiled as he pitched him the coil of frayed Manila hemp they had borrowed from a neighbor. Youseff looped it around the base of a tree, pulled the knot tight, and dropped the rest down the hole. It landed with a thud, about ten feet down, he guessed.

Youseff looked up at the blazing midday sun. It had to be almost one hundred degrees by now. Their dark eyes, dark hair, and olive skin were accustomed to the desert climate. The boys had hiked almost five miles through the Judean Desert to reach these limestone hills near the northwest corner of the Dead Sea. Caleb had discovered the crevice a week earlier while hunting with his father, who forbade him from exploring it. "You fall down there and we'll never be able to get you out," his father warned. Of course, to Caleb the warning only made the journey all the more necessary. He had, however, convinced Youseff to go first, just in case his father was right.

Youseff swung his legs down into the opening and slowly lowered himself into the dark passage. As he did, the damp, stale air filled his nostrils. "Disgusting," he said to himself as he reached the bottom and looked around.

The cave was larger than it had seemed from above. He could see a few feet in every direction, thanks mainly to the slant of high-noon sun that shone brightly through the hole in the ceiling. He took a box of matches and a candle from his pocket. The sound of the striking match echoed throughout the cavern and provided a point of illumination that grew larger once he lit the wick. After his eyes had a moment to adjust, Youseff could see that the cavern had a roughly rectangular shape about the size of the classroom that he and Caleb attended at the village school.

Youseff glanced quickly around and saw nothing out of the ordinary, or what he imagined would be ordinary for the inside of a cave, since he had never been in one. Except for a few small rocks strewn across the dusty floor, it appeared empty.

But the north end of the cave was just beyond the candle's illumination. Looking into the darkness gave him an eerie feeling. Slowly, Youseff started walking toward the shadowed section. As he did he could roughly perceive the silhouette of a mysterious object along the base of the far wall.

"What can you see?" Caleb shouted from above.

The sound of his friend's voice startled him. Youseff froze in his tracks. "Nothing yet, just dirt and rocks," he replied after regaining enough composure to answer. "But there's something over here against the wall. I can't make it out yet."

"What is it?" Caleb asked impatiently.

"Hold on a second, I'm getting there."

Youseff resumed his careful pace toward the north wall, squinting his eyes in an attempt to visualize the obscured object at its base. The further he got from the hole in the roof the more he had to depend on the candle for light. *It's probably just a pile of rocks,* he told himself. When he got within a couple feet of the object, he knelt and held the candle out in front of him.

Suddenly, he realized what it was.

# 3

"We've reached our cruising altitude of thirty-five thousand feet. I'm going to turn off the Fasten Seatbelt sign. Feel free to stretch your legs and move about the cabin."

Jack Stanton peered out the window of his first-class seat on Israeli Air's nonstop flight from Washington's Reagan airport to Jerusalem. Nothing but blue water as far as the eye could see, and not a cloud in the sky. *But a long way down*, he thought. He checked the time on his watch. *ONLY ten more hours to go.*

Patience had never been one of Jack's notable qualities, but in at least one way that had served him well.

He had been impatient as a young entrepreneur, refusing to go the traditional route of coming in at the bottom and working his way up the corporate ladder. After graduating college, he spent six months as an analyst for a D.C.-based mutual funds company. But when things didn't move fast enough for him, he broke out on his own and started an asset management firm that focused exclusively on technology stocks. And although convincing investors to take a chance on him was difficult at first, his accurate prediction of the impending tech-stock implosion made those who had gambled on him some very sizeable profits. After that, new clients had beaten down his door, and things had been nonstop ever since. What had started as a small investment house ten years ago now employed more than one hundred people, had $500 million under management, and offered assistance with mergers and acquisitions, venture capital, and commodities trading.

But now, at age thirty-three, after accomplishing most of the financial goals he had set out for himself, he had a restlessness inside him, a feeling of lack. It was if somewhere in the back of his mind loomed the uncomfortable thought: *Is this all there is?*

"Would you like a cocktail, sir?"

Jack's internal questioning was interrupted by an external one.

"No, thanks," he replied to the tall, voluptuous Israeli Air flight attendant. "How 'bout just a Diet Coke?"

"Coming right up," she said with a smile.

Jack had learned long ago that alcohol clouded his mind and was bad for business. He credited non-drinking as one of the reasons for his financial success. Women, on the other hand, had been an entirely different story.

He admired the flight attendant's long, dark hair and hourglass figure as she walked to the front of the cabin. She returned momentarily with the drink. "Here you are."

"Thanks," he said, flashing his pearly whites and revealing the small dimple on his left cheek. This was the trademark smile that had won over clients and female companions alike. He then noticed the Star of David pendant around her neck.

"This is my first time to the Holy Land," he said. "I'm really looking forward to it, but I'm a little nervous, too, with the violence and all."

"I'm sure you'll be fine, sir," she answered politely, but with a monotone voice that let him know she wasn't interested in continuing the conversation.

*Strike out*, he thought.

Then it occurred to him: Would she call Israel "the Holy Land" too? Or was that just the Christian term for it?

Jack was certainly no theologian. Catholic by birth, or a "cradle Catholic" as the term implies, he was raised by a mother who labored tirelessly at two jobs to send him and his younger sister to parochial school. Even so, he never paid as much attention to the nuances of the church as he now wished he had. Of course he understood the big picture: Jesus was the Son of God who died for our sins, rose from the dead, and is coming back later, but Jack certainly didn't have the biblical knowledge that he saw in other people. In fact, and he was careful not to advertise this, he hadn't even read the vast majority of the Christian holy book.

But that didn't mean that Jack wasn't interested in religion and philosophy. Quite the contrary, he had spent many a day grappling with such questions as "Why are we here?" and "What's the meaning of all this?" It was this philosophical side, and the unexpected feeling of lack that accompanied his material achievements, that had led him to plan this two-week trip to Israel. He hoped to rejuvenate his interest in the religion of his birth, and he hypothesized that by visiting the historic places where all the amazing events in the Bible had occurred, he could then feel a deeper, stronger connection to his faith.

And besides that, he really needed a vacation. His employees had been begging him for months to take some time off. Finally Jill, his administrative assistant, began telling all his clients in January that he would be on vacation for two weeks in August. It was June before he found out.

"Chocolate ice cream is the best!" Jack heard a young boy say insistently from across the aisle and a row behind.

"No! Vanilla!" replied an even younger-sounding girl.

"Chocolate!"

"Vanilla!"

"Chocolate!"

"Vanilla!"

Jack cocked his head around to get a look at the pair. The boy was around seven and the girl probably five or six, sitting on opposite sides of a young woman who was doing her best to ignore the conversation and continue to read her magazine.

"Mommy, tell Brian vanilla is best," the little girl whined.

The boy responded by jamming his thumbs in his ears, sticking out his tongue, and fluttering his fingers back and forth.

"That's enough," the young woman said in the motherly tone of voice that is identical in all languages, "Mia, you too."

She then calmly explained to her children that ice cream was a matter of preference, not right or wrong, and that it was entirely fine for one to like chocolate and the other to prefer vanilla. She could tell Jack had observed the commotion and leaned forward. "I hope they didn't disturb you."

"Not at all," Jack said good-naturedly. "I had a little sister too."

Witnessing their youthful interaction reminded him of another inner longing. Jack hoped to have a family one day, but except to his work, he had never been married. And it wasn't for lack of interest. He was an attractive guy, although a little on the short side. He was five foot seven, with a muscular build and sandy blond hair. And next to his genuinely likeable personality and trademark grin, his most striking characteristic was his piercing blue eyes.

Over the years there had been many dates and a few serious relationships. In the beginning, they all said they understood that running one's own business was a twenty-four-hour-a-day job, but eventually they grew tired of the last-minute cancellations, lonesome weekends, and nonexistent holidays.

Jack had always done his best to be clear about his work life from the beginning, and they all initially claimed to understand. But Jack realized, in their defense, feelings change. The problem for him was, his never had. So eventually, Jack would get the all-too-familiar ultimatum, "It's me or the job." So far, he had always chosen the job. Looking back, he hoped he had made the right choice.

Jack glanced down at his watch again. *That's the problem with long plane rides, too much time to think.*

# 4

"AHHHHHHHHH," Youseff yelled as he dropped the candle, turned around, and bolted to the dangling rope as fast as he could. Caleb jumped back from the hole, as if he expected something to shoot up and out of it.

"Get me out of here!" Youseff screamed, scurrying up the rope. Caleb quickly returned to the crevice to assist his friend.

But Youseff didn't need any help. What he had glimpsed was motivation enough to catapult his large frame up that rope in record time. Caleb quickly grabbed his arm and pulled him the rest of the way out. Youseff collapsed on the ground, looking white as a ghost and breathing heavily.

"What was it?" Caleb asked excitedly. "What did you see?"

Youseff was still trying to catch his breath. "There's a dead guy down there," he stammered in between breaths, "a skeleton."

"No way!" Caleb exclaimed as his eyes widened. "That's awesome!"

Youseff looked at him like he was out of his mind, his earlier pretense of adolescent machismo now completely discarded.

"Let's go back down and check it out!" Caleb added.

"Are you crazy?" Youseff responded, not believing his ears. The thought of reentering the cave horrified him. "Caleb, it's bad luck to disturb the dead!"

Caleb was undeterred. "That's just a silly superstition ... the guy is dead! What's he going to do to us now?"

"You are crazy!" Youseff stared in bewilderment at his friend. "I'm not going back down there!"

"Suit yourself," Caleb replied, shrugging his shoulders, "but I've got to see this."

Caleb quickly lowered himself down the rope and into the cavern. Fortunately, the candle Youseff dropped had not extinguished in the flurry. When Caleb reached the floor, he hurried toward the flickering light.

Sure enough, and to Caleb's delight, there at the base of the wall and sitting upright was a bona fide human skeleton. The flesh had long since rotted, as had most of the clothes. Caleb could make out the remnants of an old brown cloak draped around the bones. He picked up the candle from the cavern floor and ran it up and down the length of what had once been a torso.

It was then he made the second discovery of the day.

The skeleton's bony fingers were still clutching a small cylinder-shaped object to its chest. Caleb held the candle closer. The object was about twelve inches tall, six to eight inches in diameter, and made of stone. Examining it closer, he saw a ring about a half inch below the top.

*A lid*, he realized.

Outside the cavern, Youseff was beginning to worry. "Do you see it?" he called out to his friend.

Caleb was too engrossed in his discovery to answer.

"Caleb! Can you hear me?"

The second request woke Caleb from his trance. "I'm fine," he said. "The dead guy's holding something. It looks like an old stone jar."

Youseff immediately anticipated Caleb's next move. "Leave it alone, Caleb!"

Caleb laughed.

Youseff persisted. "Caleb, this guy's ghost is not going to be happy about us messing around down there, much less taking his stuff."

"Well, I'm not worried," he answered, "and besides, I don't believe in ghosts."

"Oh! That makes me feel better," Youseff replied sarcastically.

Caleb carefully peeled the bony fingers away from the jar, removing it from its resting place. He was anxious to get his find outside for further examination when it occurred to him, *How did this guy end up down here?*

He stopped and looked around the cavern. The barren cave looked the same in every place but one. A few feet from the body was a ten-foot-wide indentation in the wall. Unlike the rest of the cavern, this inset was filled with watermelon-sized rocks from bottom to top, as if they had collapsed from the ceiling above.

"I think there used to be another entrance that came out on the east side of the hill, but it looks like it caved in," Caleb shouted as he visualized the location of the former passage. He glanced back up to the hole above. "This man was trapped. He could see the daylight but couldn't get to it."

"Wonderful," Youseff answered. "I'm sure his soul is at peace."

"Don't be ridiculous, now pull this thing up." Caleb tied the rope snugly around the top of the jar, a couple of inches below the lid. "It's ready, but take it slow."

Youseff heeded the warning and carefully pulled the jar up and out. He untied the noose and dropped the rope back down to Caleb, who quickly joined him topside.

"Let's open it up," Caleb said.

"Do we have to?" Youseff pleaded.

Caleb ignored his warning. He carefully removed the lid and peered down into the container. Inside was what looked like a pair of old rolled-up newspapers. Caleb reached down and pulled out the two items. As he did, he could see that the objects inside were not newspapers at all, but something much older. He placed one on the ground next to the jar and slowly unrolled the other one. The markings on the paper were in a language he didn't recognize.

"These could be valuable ancient writings," Caleb said.

Youseff was not impressed. He crouched down to get a better look at the exposed writing. "Ohhhhhh...mumbo-jumbo, I bet that's valuable."

Caleb ignored his sarcasm. "This will be worth a lot...you'll see."

Youseff looked back at the hole in the earth. "It's not worth pissing off a ghost."

"Oh, stop being such a baby," Caleb scoffed, "and let's head back. I want to take it to the antique shop and find out what it is."

‹ℳ›

# 5

The village of Medina was a remote, dusty settlement near the northwest corner of the Dead Sea. Its wide unpaved roads were traveled more by herded animals than automobiles. Only about half of the gray cinder-block homes had indoor plumbing, and even fewer had telephones.

This was in part because the inhabitants of Medina never intended to reside here permanently. The original families who formed this community were Muslim refugees who had fled Jerusalem to avoid being caught up in the gunfire between the Israeli army and the Palestinian rebels.

Their hope was to wait out the violence and return to their homes when both sides could agree on a lasting peace.

That was in 1948. Unfortunately, they were still waiting.

By the time Caleb and Youseff reached the outskirts of Medina it was late afternoon. They hoped to skirt the perimeter of the village and take their find to the antique shop before being seen.

But their plan didn't work. Youseff's seventeen-year-old cousin, Tariq, saw them walking through the field carrying the mysterious object between them and went to investigate. Tariq had a reputation as a bully, and bumping into him was rarely a pleasant occurrence.

"What's that?" he asked the boys.

"Just an old jar we found in a cave," Youseff replied. "But don't tell anyone you saw us with it."

Tariq looked down at their bounty. "Why not?"

"Just don't, okay?" Caleb replied, annoyed. "I'll get in trouble if my father finds out I was in the caves."

Tariq realized an opportunity. "So what are you going to give me for staying quiet?"

Caleb shook his head in disgust. "Look, we found this old jar. If it's worth something and we can sell it, we'll give you some of the money."

"It doesn't look like it's worth much," Tariq snorted, as he examined the object closer. "Is there anything in it?"

Youseff started to answer when Caleb quickly cut him off. "No, nothing inside, it's empty."

Tariq sensed the awkward exchange between the two younger boys. "Let me see," he commanded as he grabbed the object, removed the lid, and looked inside.

"Nothing," he said, "and I bet that's all you get for it, too."

Caleb kept his poker face. They had hidden the scrolls in an old hollow tree about ten minutes prior to their encounter with Tariq. One of the things they had learned growing up in a depressed area was to always hide your valuables.

"You're probably right," Caleb replied, "but I still hope you'll keep it a secret."

"Look, kid, I've got better things to do with my time than keep track of you for your parents," Tariq said sternly, "but if you do get some money for that thing, I better get some of it, or they will find out."

"Sure," Caleb said coolly.

As he finished speaking, the trio could hear the Islamic call to prayer echoing in the distance from the loudspeaker at the village mosque.

"Oh, no," Youseff said hurriedly, "we'll never make it in time for evening prayers."

Tariq smirked. "I wouldn't waste my time."

"You mustn't say that, Tariq," Youseff admonished him.

Tariq just ignored him. He turned and began walking away from the village.

When he was out of earshot, Caleb offered his opinion of Youseff's cousin, "What a jerk."

"I know. I'm glad you thought to hide the scrolls, but we should have hidden the jar, too."

"No," replied Caleb. "We need something to show the old man. Then maybe he can tell us what we have found."

They continued unnoticed along the outskirts of the village until they came to the only antique and souvenir shop in Medina. The store survived by turning a meager profit from the few tourists who were brave enough to venture off the West Bank's more traveled roads in hopes of finding better bargains.

The proprietor was an elderly man, born in Egypt, who simultaneously scared and intrigued the village youth. Local legend maintained he had once been an officer in the Egyptian army and had fought against the Jews in the 1960s war. Forgotten by most of the adults in the community, he kept to himself but would often excite the younger boys by telling yarns about his battles against the "Zionist invaders."

As they expected, the old man was sitting in a rocking chair on the store's front porch. He spotted the duo and the unusual object they were carrying. "Hello, lads, what's that you have there?"

"Well, sir, I was hoping you could tell us," Caleb replied.

The boys sat the jar on the porch in front of him. The old man got out of his chair and knelt to examine it.

After studying the object carefully for a moment, he pointed to the lid. "May I?"

"Of course," said Caleb.

He removed the lid and looked inside, seeing that it was empty.

"Where did you get this?" he asked.

"We found it in a cave in the desert," Youseff said.

He looked at both boys inquisitively. "In a cave. That's exciting. I'm sure your mother and father would be pleased to hear you were running around in the caves. Are your parents encouraging that these days?"

"No, sir," said Caleb.

"Well," the old man said, "let's get it out of sight then. You can leave it here until you decide what to do with it."

Relieved, they picked up the jar and followed him inside. The store was small, and contained the variety of knickknacks one would expect in an antique and gift shop. There was a weathered-looking stand of old books, some small pieces of antique furniture, and a glass display case that housed an array of handmade Palestinian jewelry. Another case displayed a variety of pens, T-shirts, and hats with the embossed phrase "Free Palestine Now."

"Can you tell us if this old vase is worth anything?" Youseff asked as they entered.

"Everything is worth something," said the old man. "Set it here on the counter so I can look at it again."

The boys did as instructed.

"Do you have any idea what it is?" Caleb asked.

"Possibly," he replied thoughtfully. "The remains of a two-thousand-year-old Jewish community were found in the caves not far from here some fifty or sixty years ago. I knew some of the people who helped on the archeological excavation. This jar looks similar to the pottery items they unearthed."

"Wow," said Youseff excitedly, "so it is valuable!"

"Well," the old man said hesitantly, trying to calm their enthusiasm, "I'm only speculating. I have no idea if what you found is the same type of thing or not. And besides, they found lots of this type of pottery. So although I am sure it is worth something, it won't fetch a briefcase full of money."

His last remark deflated the boys' spirits.

"Was *anything* found there worth any value?" Youseff asked.

"Yes," replied the old man. "But it wasn't gold or silver or anything like that. There were several religious scrolls found in some of the caves, inside jars like this one. These writings turned out to be of importance to the Jews and Christians. They called them the Dead Sea Scrolls."

Fortunately the old man was still examining the jar, otherwise he would have seen Youseff's eyes grow as big as saucers. Caleb was about to fill him in on the day's discoveries when the old man added, "But if you were to find something of that magnitude, I'm afraid there would be other bad news."

His comment caught Caleb off guard. "What do you mean?" he asked.

"All archaeological finds of that type are considered property of the state, and by law they must be turned over to the Israeli authorities."

"You've got to be kidding," Caleb blurted.

Youseff was just as shocked. "That's not fair!"

The ferocity of their reactions surprised the old man. "Oh, I wouldn't be too worried just yet. No one will notice if another clay vase pops up for sale in an antique shop…but one of those scrolls, now that's a different story."

The boys were speechless. Caleb's heart sank. *Could it be that they had found something of great value and they would not be able to profit from it?*

By now the old man realized they were hiding something from him. "Of course," he offered, "if you did find anything that would be of interest to the Israelis, there is always the possibility of a quiet sale."

"A quiet sale?" Caleb asked. "What does that mean?"

"Let's just say that this would be a transaction undertaken without the knowledge of the Israeli government, and for that reason it would have to be kept very quiet, because if they ever found out, there would be severe consequences for everyone involved." The old man's intonation grew more stern with each word.

"So how much would one of those scrolls bring in a private sale?" Caleb inquired.

The old man smiled. "Why, did you find one?"

Caleb didn't immediately answer the question. He looked over at Youseff in a way that intimated for him to keep quiet, too. "No," he finally responded, "but I'd like to know just in case we do."

"Very well," the old man replied cordially, choosing not to press the issue for now. "If one should turn up, I'll see if I can get a price for you. And in the meantime, your jar will be safe with me until you decide what to do with it."

The boys thanked him again and left, still dumbstruck by the latest revelation.

Once they were outside, Youseff said, "I can't believe it! Those damn things are valuable, and we're supposed to hand them over to the Jews."

"I know," agreed Caleb, equally frustrated. "They've taken everything from us, and now this, too?"

Despair overtook them both.

"But maybe we should just hand them over and forget about it," Youseff said fearfully. "I don't want any trouble."

"What?" Caleb was angry. "Youseff, giving them to the Israelis is not an option! I would throw them back down in that cave before doing that!"

"Well, what do you think we should do?" Youseff asked. "I don't like the sound of that quiet sale, because if someone finds out, we could get in big trouble. We've all heard the horrible stories about the Israeli prisons!"

Caleb squinted his eyes and thought hard. "A private sale might be all right," he reasoned.

"I don't know," Youseff countered cautiously.

Caleb's face illuminated as he formed an idea. "Maybe we can sell them ourselves!"

Youseff looked at him blankly. "How are we going to do that? We don't know anyone who would want to buy them."

"Don't be ridiculous!" Caleb chastised. "We could sell them at one of the tourist areas and they could never trace it back to us. I bet we could get ten or twenty dollars American! We'd be rich!"

Despite the many stories Youseff had heard about the risks of crossing the Israeli government, he realized that Caleb had a point. The potential for getting caught was low, and he didn't want to be left out of any proceeds. Still, he was unsure. "I don't know, Caleb. Let's think about it overnight."

As the boys made their way down the dusty street, the old man had been carefully watching their departure from the front window of his shop. Confident that they were far enough away, he quickly headed to the pay phone in the center of the town.

# 6

As his plane landed in Jerusalem, Jack thought of the other reason he had chosen the Holy Land as his destination.

Punjeeh Kohli.

Punjeeh was Jack's old college roommate. Born in India, Punjeeh had come to the United States at age eighteen to pursue his education. Although they both had chosen a small state school in rural southwestern Virginia, Jack went there because it was inexpensive, whereas Punjeeh went on a full academic scholarship. A stroke of fate landed them in the same dorm room, where they quickly became close friends. And considering the differences in their backgrounds and personalities, this was a bit of an oddity.

For instance, where Jack was aggressive and outspoken, Punjeeh was easygoing and quiet. And whereas Jack got involved in every intramural sport the college offered, Punjeeh considered such activities "nonsense." As far as grades and campus life were concerned, Jack was quite satisfied to slide by with Cs and an occasional B, but was one of the most well-known students on campus. Punjeeh, meanwhile, had little interest in campus social activities but graduated summa cum laude with a degree in biology and then went on to medical school.

On the outside, they had little in common. But on the inside, they were like brothers. They had both come from humble beginnings, both were focused on making something out of themselves, and consequently, they both enjoyed fighting for the underdog.

This last similarity became evident to Punjeeh his freshman year when he was confronted by three drunk local boys while walking alone just off-campus one evening. They started screaming, "Hey, darky," and throwing beer cans at him. Punjeeh ignored them, walked faster, and was trying to get back to his dorm as quickly as possible. Suddenly, he felt a hand on his shoulder as one of his assailants spun him around and shouted, "Hey, Gandhi! I'm talking to you!"

Punjeeh didn't have a chance to answer before Jack came flying out of nowhere and leveled the assailant. While local boy number one lay dazed and bewildered, Jack quickly turned to the other two.

"Who's next?" he asked.

Both turned and ran.

Jack looked back at Punjeeh, who was standing there somewhat amazed and very much relieved.

"Don't worry, Gandhi," Jack said with a grin, "I didn't take a non-violence pledge."

Jack had wanted to turn the incident over to campus police, but Punjeeh would have none of it. "They've had enough embarrassment for one night," he said. "Let's go home."

Another thing Jack and Punjeeh shared was their Catholic up-bringing, except that while Punjeeh never missed a Sunday mass in their four years of college, church was the one place on campus Jack was virtually unknown.

Jack remembered initially being surprised Punjeeh was Catholic, but Punjeeh explained that Christianity had a long history in India. To start, there was a legendary tale among Indians that during the biblically unaccounted-for time in Jesus' life, roughly between ages twelve and thirty, he was in India. "Where else would he have learned all those great stories?" Punjeeh quizzed Jack jokingly.

Punjeeh was also well-versed in Catholic doctrine. Jack often said that he learned more about Catholicism from his four years living with Punjeeh than he had in the previous twelve years of Catholic school.

For instance, it was Punjeeh who explained that for the first several hundred years after Jesus' life, to be a Christian in the West was synonymous with being Roman Catholic. "The apostle Peter was the equivalent of the first pope, the head of the Christian church in Rome," Punjeeh had once told him. "There was no other Christian church in the West but the Catholic one for hundreds of years. Every Protestant denomination, Methodist, Lutheran, Episcopalian, Baptist, etc., was an offshoot, directly or indirectly, from the Roman Catholic Church."

After college, Jack started his business and Punjeeh went off to medical school, where he met Esther, a Jewish medical student from Israel. Despite the differences in their religious upbringing, they fell deeply in love and were married four years later. Jack was his best man. After graduation and residency, Punjeeh agreed to move with her to Israel, where he was now an ER doctor.

Even though they were an ocean apart, Jack and Punjeeh had always stayed in close contact, exchanging emails and transatlantic phone calls. But over the past few months, Jack detected a change in Punjeeh. In some ways, Punjeeh seemed more relaxed, more at ease, but he also seemed disconnected, distant. For instance, when Jack explained that he was becoming more interested in Catholicism, Punjeeh seemed unmoved. The last time they spoke, Punjeeh made the comment that living in the Holy Land had opened his eyes to some things. Jack had asked him to elaborate, but Punjeeh said they would discuss it when he arrived.

Jack made his way through customs and headed for the airport exit when he heard a familiar voice.

"Jack, over here."

Jack turned around to see the dark bushy eyebrows of his friend's smiling face.

"Hey, buddy," Jack replied as he exchanged a bear hug with the slightly taller Punjeeh. "You haven't aged a bit."

"God, it's good to see you, man! So glad you came," Punjeeh replied jubilantly.

"Me too, it's been too long. And how is Esther?"

"She is quite well, thank you. But, you poor devil, you will not see her tonight. She is visiting her sister in Tel Aviv and won't be home until tomorrow."

"So it will be the two of us for a little while," Jack replied with a smile, "just like old times."

They reminisced about their college days and their current busy work schedules as they walked through the terminal to Punjeeh's car. It was 8 p.m. when his plane landed, and he had been so focused on Punjeeh that Jack had forgotten for a moment that he was in a foreign country. This changed the moment he stepped outside. Although the darkness prevented him from seeing much farther than the airport parking lot, Jack's sense of smell immediately reminded him he wasn't stateside anymore. The night air in Jerusalem had a fragrance that he had never experienced. There was a hint of old in the smell, but not old in a bad way. This was an antique smell, and with it came the feeling that he was on historic ground.

They loaded Jack's luggage into Punjeeh's silver BMW 535i sedan and set out for his apartment. The airport was in a rural section of town, but once they got onto the main highway Jack could see the lights of downtown Jerusalem in the distance. Buildings of all shapes and sizes dotted the rolling hills as far as he could see. A variety of low-growing trees densely peppered the landscape and provided an interesting juxtaposition of old and new. The sheer vastness of this civilization set amongst bountiful hills reminded him of the north side of Los Angeles, the noteworthy exception being the ancient ambiance the environment here exuded, in many ways the antithesis of LA.

"We're not far," Punjeeh said as he gunned the engine. "And traffic shouldn't be too bad this time of night."

"Didn't you tell me that you live in the old section of town?"

"Yes, and it's not just the old section, it's literally called 'the Old City.' It's what this city is famous for, as practically every street corner is historically significant for Christians, Muslims, or Jews."

"Please, fill me in," Jack said, remembering how knowledgeable Punjeeh was in religious matters, and that he just needed an inquisitor to get him started.

"For Christians, there's the Church of the Holy Sepulchre, which they say houses the place where Jesus was crucified and the tomb where his body was placed."

"Yes," Jack marveled in anticipation, "I want to see that first."

"And for the Jews, the Western Wall is the most sacred of all places. It is the only section of foundation that remains from the Temple Mount, where their sacred temple was built more than three thousand years ago. Unfortunately it was destroyed by the Romans during the first century AD and never rebuilt. That's why, today, the Western Wall is also called the Wailing Wall, as Jews are still in misery over the destruction of their temple."

"Why don't they just rebuild it now?" Jack asked curiously.

"If it were only that easy ... Remember that Jerusalem was later ruled by the Muslims, who also have a religious claim to the Temple Mount ... they believe it was here that the prophet Muhammad rode up to heaven on the back of a great stallion ... and to commemorate his ascension, the Muslims built a magnificent blue stone mosque with a golden dome on top, called the Dome of the Rock."

"I've seen pictures of that," Jack remembered. "It looks fantastic."

"It is quite an impressive work of architecture," Punjeeh agreed, "but it has also been a source of bad blood with the Jews for centuries, as they considered it an insult to have a mosque built right where their sacred temple once stood."

"I can see their point," Jack grimaced.

"Yes, family feuds are the worst."

Jack vaguely remembered that there was a religious connection between Jews and Muslims, but couldn't remember how the pieces fit together. "That's right," he said, "isn't there some ancient ancestry between the two groups?"

"Yes, Islam and Judaism are religious first cousins, so to speak," Punjeeh replied. "Both trace their roots back to Abraham of the Old Testament. Remember that in the Old Testament, God asked Abraham to sacrifice his son, supposedly right here on the Temple Mount in the Old City. Both religions agree on that much, but that's where a fork in the road emerges."

"What do you mean?"

"Judaism maintains that God asked Abraham to sacrifice his son Isaac. Muslims insist that God instructed Abraham to sacrifice his other son, Ishmael. Whoever it was, God stopped Abraham just before he was about to drive a dagger through his son's abdomen."

"Okay," said Jack, "I remember this story now."

"Good," said Punjeeh. "Then you also remember that God told Abraham that because he was willing to sacrifice his own son, he showed his faith and trust in God, and God then promised to bless Abraham's offspring as a result of his loyalty.

"Jews and Christians claim to be descendants of Abraham via Isaac. Muslims claim Muhammad was a descendant of Abraham via Ishmael. So members of each religion believe themselves to be the beneficiaries of God's promise to Abraham—or that the Holy Land belongs to them—and that's the biggest reason for all their trouble."

They turned the corner just as Punjeeh finished his last sentence, and Jack couldn't help but be distracted by the structure in front of him. A huge sand-colored stone wall approximately forty feet high stretched as far as he could see in each direction.

Punjeeh sensed his surprise. "And here we are," he said, "the Old City. It's completely encircled by a rock wall that was built centuries ago to keep the city safe from invaders."

A couple hundred yards later they veered to the right and slowed down as they approached a gap in the towering enclosure.

"The Jaffa Gate," Punjeeh noted.

Within seconds of entering the Old City, the streets narrowed significantly and three- and four-story buildings came right up to sidewalks. Most of the stores were closed, the cafes being the exception.

Punjeeh made an immediate right into the Ha-Kardo section, which housed most of the Old City's Jewish inhabitants. He pulled the car over and parked in front of a row of clothing shops.

"Here we are, 888 Joshua Avenue. Our apartment is upstairs."

They grabbed Jack's luggage out of the back, entered a nondescript door between two of the shops, and made their way up narrow stairs to the entrance of Punjeeh's apartment. Once inside, Jack was impressed with the spaciousness, as the apartment appeared to take up the entire second floor.

Although the building itself was very old, the interior of the apartment had been extensively remodeled. The floors were a wide-planked distressed hardwood, and their dark-brown color was complemented by the light-tan stucco walls. The ceilings were ten feet high in all rooms except in the main living and dining area, where a twenty-foot vaulted ceiling was accented by rustic wood rafters spaced approximately every six feet for the length of the room.

And while the remodeled apartment maintained an old-world feel, the furnishings were distinctly modern. Vibrantly colored abstract paintings adorned the walls, the sofas were shiny black leather, and in the dining area sat a six-foot-round glass table on a white marble pedestal.

"Very posh, Punjeeh," said Jack with a wink.

"It's no mansion on the Potomac, but we like it," Punjeeh joked, referring to the 10,000-square-foot home just outside Washington, D.C., that Jack had purchased a couple of years ago.

"Hey, the place was a steal in our depressed market," Jack said defensively and shrugged his shoulders. "I'll sell it for twice what I paid in five years."

Punjeeh laughed at his response. "My dear Jack, remember that you don't have to make excuses with me for who you are. I will always encourage you to follow your heart, to hell with what other people say."

Jack was glad to hear that at least that part of his friend's character hadn't changed. Punjeeh gave him a tour of the apartment, showing Jack the master bedroom, two additional bedrooms, a quaint study, and an oversized kitchen. But it wasn't until they concluded the tour that Jack realized what he hadn't seen in Punjeeh's apartment: a crucifix or any other Catholic iconography.

And while this absence wouldn't be noteworthy in many Catholic homes, the opposite was so when it came to Punjeeh. Jack remembered that in college Punjeeh insisted on hanging a crucifix and a picture of Pope John Paul II in their dorm room, even though Jack had tried desperately to dissuade him, as he was afraid it would be a deterrent for the late-night activities he enjoyed with female friends. But Punjeeh refused to relent. Later, when Punjeeh and Esther discussed marriage, Jack remembered how they had agreed that both would be able to display icons of their respective faiths.

"Where's your crucifix?" Jack asked pointedly.

The question seemed to catch Punjeeh off guard, but he recovered quickly. "Oh … uhh … I think it got lost in the move. I haven't had a chance to replace it," he replied nonchalantly.

Jack wasn't letting him off that easy. "Punjeeh!" he exclaimed. "You've never lived anywhere that you didn't hang a crucifix. Now what the hell is going on with you?"

Punjeeh bellowed with laughter. "Okay, so you're not buying that one? My friend, it's too late to have that conversation tonight. Can we talk about it tomorrow?"

Jack remembered that he hadn't slept in more than twenty-four hours and acquiesced. "Okay, tomorrow it will have to be."

"Good," Punjeeh replied, "and perhaps we can take a ride out through the Judean Desert to the Dead Sea as well, where the healing waters can rejuvenate your tired and overworked bones."

"The Dead Sea – that doesn't sound very rejuvenating," Jack replied with his trademark grin, "but you know me, I'll try anything once."

*7*

"An ancient letter from the Gnostics," Punjeeh exclaimed, "what a find, Jack!"

Jack stared blankly across the desk at Chloe, Punjeeh, and Professor King. He was really feeling like a first grader in this group. Finally he had to ask, "So who the heck were these guhnostiks?" He deliberately pronounced the silent G.

Chloe smiled understandingly. "That's a good question, Jack, as very few people outside of the academic world have ever heard of the Gnostic Christians. And it's probably easiest to explain the Gnostics by contrasting them to the other early Christian movement, the Literalists, as they were the group who later became the Roman Catholic Church."

"Excellent idea, my dear Chloe, please continue," beamed Professor King.

Jack and Punjeeh remained silent, eagerly awaiting her explanation.

"Most people in the West have the mistaken impression that the Christian Church was a unified force from the time of Jesus and his disciples right up to the Protestant Reformation in 1517."

Punjeeh and Jack exchanged glances. That was the historical version they had learned.

"But that's just not the case," she continued, "at least not for the first three hundred years or so, as there was actually a handful of different Christian movements in the beginning, each with varying theological ideas, but they more or less fell into one of two groups: Gnostic or Literalist. And unfortunately for the Gnostics, the differences between the two groups proved to be too big for one religion."

"What were some of the differences?" Punjeeh asked.

"The cornerstone of Literalist Christianity was *belief*," Chloe answered. "Namely, belief in Jesus Christ. In their eyes, all one had to do to be a good Christian was believe in the divinity of Jesus, be baptized, and follow the direction of church officials. Membership was very simple and straightforward. If a believer followed these precepts, he or she would be rewarded with heaven in the afterlife."

Punjeeh chuckled. "This is undoubtedly the group that became the Catholics, because not much has changed."

Jack was still confused about something. "So why were they called the Literalists?"

"Another good question, Jack," Chloe replied. "And the answer gets back to their beliefs. As you know from your own religious education, the Catholic Church assumes a very literal position regarding the Gospels of Matthew, Mark, Luke, John, and the Acts of the Apostles. They understand them to be actual historical accounts of the events in the life of Jesus of Nazareth and his disciples. Of the two early Christian movements, the Literalists were the ones who originally advocated the idea that the gospels were historically infallible, hence they were referred to as the Literalists."

Her response triggered another question from Jack. "Do you mean to suggest that the Gnostics didn't share that view?"

"In contrast to the strict beliefs of the Literalists," she answered, "the Gnostics said that belief in the historical accuracy of the gospels was not as important as understanding the inner meaning of Jesus' teachings."

Professor King interrupted, "You see, gentlemen, the word *Gnostic* is a Greek term. It comes from the word *gnosis*, which means 'to know.' Definitively speaking, a Gnostic is 'one who knows.'"

"Knows what?" Jack asked and shrugged his shoulders.

"According to them," Professor King continued, "*knows God*. The Gnostics claim to have *special knowledge of God*."

Jack and Punjeeh's expressions signaled they were unclear on what Professor King meant, and Chloe recognized it.

"Experience may be a better way of putting it," she offered. "The Gnostics wanted to experience God. Their understanding of Christianity was very esoteric. They were more concerned with the inner meaning of Christ's teachings. Unlike the Literalists, who taught that belief in Jesus' divinity and death on the cross was the key to salvation and a rewarding afterlife, the Gnostics taught that belief was just the beginning of the spiritual path, not the end. For them, knowing or experiencing God *in this lifetime* was the ultimate aim. "

"And when the Gnostic adherent achieved this experience of God," said Professor King, "he or she was said to have realized *gnosis*."

"That sounds very mystical," Punjeeh remarked. "It reminds me of the Buddhist concept of Enlightenment."

"Similar I think, yes," Professor King concurred.

"I'm not following what they meant by 'knowing or experiencing God,'" Jack said skeptically. "How does one do that?"

Chloe bit her lower lip as she searched for another way to explain. "Let me give you an example that a professor gave me when I first studied the Gnostics. You've heard of Einstein's Theory of Relativity, right? $E=mc^2$?"

"Sure," said Jack.

"Great! And would you mind explaining its major points to me then, please?"

Jack frowned. "Uhhh…no," he said and grinned. "I don't know that much about it."

"But based on the fact that Einstein was a brilliant scientist, you believe that his theory is probably valid, right?" she continued.

"Okay, yeah, sure," Jack replied, wondering where this was going.

"Now contrast your belief in Einstein's theory of relativity with your knowledge of a simple mathematical formula; say, one plus one equals two."

Jack thought about it for a moment. "Okay…" he said hesitantly, still puzzled.

Chloe's expression turned more serious. "Now which one of these mathematical theories do you *believe*, and which one do you *know*?"

That's when it clicked for Jack. "Okay, I think I get it. I don't need to believe that one plus one is two, I *know* that. But in regard to Einstein's theory, I am just taking his word for it."

"Exactly," said Chloe. "In a way, you've experienced one formula, while the other you are simply choosing to believe."

"And carrying the analogy to Gnostic principles even further," said Professor King," if you spent years studying physics, it's possible that you could know that $E=mc^2$ the same way you now know that one plus one equals two."

Jack grinned, "Well, thank you, Professor, but I'm not so sure that would be possible."

Chloe and Professor King laughed.

Meanwhile, the seeker in Punjeeh was becoming increasingly intrigued by the Gnostic's philosophy. "Please tell us more about these Gnostics. How else were they different from the Literalists, those who later became the Roman Catholics?"

"For starters," Chloe began, "there were some practical differences between the Gnostics and the Literalists. As the Gnostics were devoid of any hierarchal structure, they had no permanent priestly class. Instead, they took turns blessing communion, performing baptisms, marriages, and the like. As you know, this is quite the opposite of the Literalist church, who instituted a continuous priestly class that has survived via the Roman Catholic Church to the present day."

She took a drink from the coffee cup on her desk before continuing.

"And the Gnostics' view on women in the church was very egalitarian as well. They did not discriminate on the basis of sex. Women were welcome to serve in all capacities in a Gnostic church. Unfortunately, the Literalists' position on women in the church then is virtually identical to the Catholic Church's position today."

Jack detected more than a hint of antipathy in her last comment.

"And all of these practices underlined the primary Gnostic principal that *everyone has equal access to God*. They taught that there was no need for an intermediary, unlike the Literalists, who maintained that access to God could only be achieved through their priests and bishops."

"If all of the early Christian churches had become Gnostic instead of Catholic," Professor King summarized, "the clergy would have been out of business."

"Well, we couldn't have that now, could we?" Punjeeh replied sarcastically.

"There were also differences in theology," Chloe resumed, "some of which you may find rather hard to understand. For instance, while the Literalist Christians accepted and worshiped Jehovah, the God of the Old Testament, many of the Gnostics wanted nothing to do with him, as they saw Jehovah as a pseudo-God, or a false God."

Jack was aghast. "A pseudo-God?"

"It may seem strange to us now," Professor King interjected, "since the Literalists' message eventually triumphed, but remember that in the Old Testament, Jehovah is often portrayed as an angry, jealous God that routinely punishes his followers for their mistakes and does even worse things to his enemies. The Gnostics believed this was quite the opposite of Jesus' teachings of love and forgiveness for everyone, and they could not reconcile Jesus' message with the behavior of the God of the Old Testament."

"You mean the Gnostics disapproved of a God who would ask someone to sacrifice their own son in order to prove his faith, like Jehovah did with Abraham?" Punjeeh asked.

"That's one good example," Chloe agreed. "And the Gnostics maintained that Jehovah's behavior in many parts of the Old Testament was completely incompatible with the true nature of God. They claimed that the real God was an ineffable, omnipotent, all-loving being that by the very definition of the word 'God' could not possess the flawed human characteristics Jehovah did, namely vanity, fear, vengefulness, and the like."

The room fell silent for a moment as Jack and Punjeeh reflected on this Gnostic idea.

"An ego," said Punjeeh thoughtfully. "God could not have an ego."

"Very good, Punjeeh," said Chloe, impressed by his insight. "The Gnostics argued that it was impossible for God to possess what we would call in modern-day terminology *the ego*, or what they called the *lower self*. You see, the Gnostics taught that human beings were made up of two parts, a higher self and a lower self. They wrote that the lower self, or the ego, is the part of the human psyche that gets angry, jealous, fearful, vengeful, and the like, while their description of the higher self is more akin to what we might call the human soul or spirit, and is the part of us that loves, forgives, and practices kindness and understanding. According to the Gnostics, the higher self desires only peace and is the part of human beings that is eternal, or does not die."

She paused to let her words sink in.

"Because most central to Gnostic philosophy is the idea that we are all connected, that we are all part of God, or 'The One Life.'"

"The One what?" Jack asked, not sure he had heard her correctly.

"'The One Life,'" she repeated, "which for them was something akin to the essence of life, a Divine spark or life force that is inside each human being. The Gnostics wrote that The One Life was the true God, an ineffable, all-powerful consciousness that was neither male nor female, and all human beings are part of The One Life via the higher self."

Chloe could see the skepticism on Jack's face. "Please don't misunderstand what I am saying. The Gnostics didn't claim we were physically connected, but rather that there is an unseen inner or spiritual connectedness between all human beings."

"I do say, Chloe, that was an excellent characterization," chimed in Professor King. "A central component of Gnosticism was that God is inside each and every human being. And if you don't mind, Chloe, I want to add to something you said about the ego."

"Of course, Professor, please."

"Gentlemen," said Professor King, looking at Jack and Punjeeh, "the Gnostics also taught that the lower self, or the ego, was the reason why human beings experience suffering."

"Come again?" Jack said.

Professor King smiled. "This is one of the more difficult concepts to grasp, but in short, the Gnostics maintained that the ego was the only part of the human psyche that suffers. And when they used the word *suffering*, they did not mean physical pain, but rather internal or psychological suffering."

"I'm not sure I'm following you," Jack repeated. "What's the difference between pain and suffering?"

"Good point, Jack," Professor King responded with a chuckle. "When I say pain, I really mean physical pain only, like when you have a toothache, or your back is sore, etc. There is no necessary psychological aspect to that type of discomfort; it just hurts."

Punjeeh grinned. "Ahh, so you mean the type of pain someone should see a doctor for—"

Professor King chuckled again. "Quite right, Dr. Punjeeh. And unlike physical pain, when the Gnostics referred to suffering, they meant something that can only happen in the mind. Specifically, the Gnostics taught that suffering occurs every time you fight or resist circumstances that are beyond your control."

"That's sometimes a subtle distinction," Punjeeh said thoughtfully. "As the type of mental suffering you describe could come about from something simple…maybe even complaining about the rain then, right?"

"That's an excellent example, Dr. Punjeeh," the professor replied enthusiastically, "as how many times do we let something as uncontrollable as the rain *ruin the day*, so to speak, without understanding that it was not the rain that caused the problem, but our reaction to it."

Jack dissented. "I think it's a bit of a stretch to call complaining about the rain a form of human suffering," he scoffed.

"Perhaps," Professor King replied good-naturedly, "but I wouldn't let the trivial nature of that example fool you, as the Gnostics taught that objection to events beyond our control was at the root of all psychological suffering. And the crux of their teaching was that the ego is the only part of us that participates in this type of futile resistance effort, no matter the gravity of the situation, and it is the only part of us to experience the suffering that comes about by this resistance. Because unlike the higher self or spirit, which knows that life always unfolds exactly as it is supposed to, a key component of the ego is its tendency to fight and resist events beyond its control."

Jack considered Professor King's words for a moment. He wondered how useful this philosophy was in the real world.

"But on the bright side," Professor King continued, "the Gnostics taught that when the individual's ego dies, all suffering dies with it, and that this was the true meaning of Jesus' teaching when he said that his followers '*must die to themselves and be born again.*' The Gnostics maintained it was not a bodily death that Jesus was referring to, but the death of the lower self or ego."

"And as best we can tell," Chloe added, "the death of the ego was what happened when the Gnostic adherent experienced gnosis, after which, only the higher self would remain. And for them, the higher self is the part of us that is connected, and the sum total of our higher selves is equivalent to God, or The One Life I mentioned a moment ago."

"So let me get this straight," Jack said, still trying to understand. "The Gnostics equated this One Life theory with God, and they believed that each one of us contains a little piece of God."

"Precisely," spoke up Professor King. "And they would point to the Gospel of Luke for validation, to the line where Jesus says 'the Kingdom of God is within you.'"

# 8

*1 Day Earlier–Morning*

Still jetlagged from the night before, Jack awoke to the sound of church bells ringing in the distance. It took him a few seconds to remember where he was. *Ah yes … Israel*, he thought. He jumped out of bed, got dressed, and went to look for Punjeeh.

But instead of finding his friend, he found a note on the kitchen counter.

*Jack,*

*It's 4 a.m. and I just got a call from the hospital. I'm sorry I won't be able to join you sightseeing this morning. I've left you a tourist map of the Old City. I should be home by noon, then we can head to the Dead Sea—*

*Punjeeh*

Jack was only a bit disappointed. He kind of liked the idea of exploring the Old City alone. He found some coffee and blueberry bagels, a breakfast ritual Punjeeh had retained from their college days.

After eating and making a careful study of the map, Jack set out for his day's adventure. As he exited the apartment building, he marveled at the sights and smells of the Old City. Jerusalem had an international flavor that was unlike anything he had ever experienced. Shops advertised the sale of Kosher and Halal meat, local art and jewelry, and a variety of religious souvenirs.

The people were equally diverse. There were Muslim women whose bodies were veiled from head to toe, Hasidic Jewish men in all black with beards and bowler-style hats, and Christian monks wearing leather sandals and dark-brown robes.

Jack navigated the narrow sandstone streets for about fifteen minutes before arriving at Christianity's holiest site: the Church of the Holy Sepulchre.

Believed by many to be built on the site of Jesus' crucifixion and entombment, the mammoth structure looked to Jack more like a medieval castle than a church. About four to five stories high, its arched windows and heavy wooden doors stood incased by sand-colored rock weathered from centuries of exposure. Capping the structure was a magnificent dome with a life-sized gold cross.

As Jack walked through the doors, he was awed by the beautiful tile floors, arched doorways, and colorful mosaics adorning the walls. He looked around for a few minutes when a church spokesman announced that a guided tour was just beginning. Jack decided to tag along.

He followed the group of about twenty people down to a chamber that glittered with gold and silver gem-studded crosses, a marble altar, and hundreds of burning candles. Directly behind the altar, a life-sized crucifix rose from a sterling-silver platform. The sculpture of Jesus that hung on the cross was so detailed that he actually looked alive.

"You are standing on the rock of Golgotha, right where Jesus was crucified," said the dark-skinned guide in a thick Mediterranean accent.

Jack felt nauseated as he listened to the guide explain the crucifixion process.

"He would have watched as the Roman soldiers drove nails through his wrists and feet. As they lifted the cross and placed it in the ground, the weight of his body would have torn away at the flesh around the spikes. Finally, they pierced his side with a spear to hasten his death."

The guide then pointed to a silver disk embedded in the tile floor directly under the altar. "This is where the cross was erected," he said. "This is where Jesus hung from the cross and gave his own life for our sins."

A wave of guilt swept over Jack. The idea that Jesus died for our sins was the main aspect of the Church's teachings he didn't understand. As a young child entering parochial school, he remembered being scared and confused when he first encountered the crucifix. *What did I do that was so bad that someone had to die for it?*

Jack knew this story had a happy ending, he wanted to get to it. He followed the group to the centerpiece of the church, a majestic rotunda that was as wide as a football field and directly under the huge dome he had seen from the outside. In the middle of the rotunda was an ornately decorated free-standing stone building. White candles in large gold candleholders illuminated both sides of the entrance. A line of people waited to get inside. "There it is," the guide said, pointing at the building, "the tomb of our Lord Jesus Christ."

Jack couldn't believe he was here. While standing in line and waiting for a chance to view the tomb, he remembered the central message of Christianity he had learned as a young boy: his body was laid to rest in a tomb, but on the third day Jesus rose from the dead.

After several minutes passed, Jack was finally able to enter the sanctuary. It was divided into two rooms. The first was a large vestibule, with elaborate carvings on the walls of angels, crosses, and other Christian iconography.

On the opposite side of the entrance was the doorway to the second room, which was roped off by the red velvet restraints common at any movie theater. Visitors were allowed only to peer inside.

Jack inched his way slowly toward the doorway to get a look. When he finally got close enough to see inside, he shuddered at the body-sized stone slab before him. *This is it*, he thought to himself, overwhelmed with emotion as he contemplated how Jesus' body had once lain on the spot right in front of him. He closed his eyes, said a silent prayer, and genuflected toward the stone slab while making the sign of the cross over his forehead, torso, and shoulders.

He looked over his shoulder and saw the long line of people waiting behind him. Remembering that Punjeeh would be coming home soon, he decided to head back.

\* \* \*

It was one o'clock by the time Jack made it to the apartment. He found Punjeeh relaxing on the sofa, still in his hospital scrubs.

"How was your experience in the Old City this morning?" Punjeeh asked.

"Unbelievable," Jack replied excitedly. "I toured the Church of the Holy Sepulchre, saw where Christ was crucified, and his tomb. It was a very moving experience."

Punjeeh started to say something, then stopped himself. Instead, he politely offered, "It certainly has that effect on people."

Jack was struck immediately by Punjeeh's tone. It was the same detachment that had caused concern in Jack the past few months. Punjeeh had never been good at hiding his true feelings, and Jack could tell there was something else he really wanted to say.

But before he could ask him about it, Punjeeh changed the subject, "Tell me, my friend, shall we go to the Dead Sea so you can rejuvenate your tired, overworked bones in its healing waters?"

"Sounds great."

"Let us go now before it gets too late. Esther wants us home for dinner, and she is having a girlfriend over she wants you to meet."

"Oh, really," Jack said, pleasantly surprised. "An attractive girlfriend?"

"Chloe is a very attractive woman," Punjeeh said hesitantly, "but I'm afraid she's not your type."

"Why, is she gay?" Jack shot back, sensing Punjeeh was setting him up.

"No, no, it's worse than that–she's an intellectual," Punjeeh said, howling with laughter. "If she were gay, you might have a chance!"

"Very funny," Jack quipped.

Punjeeh grinned. "She's a friend of Esther's from Greece, a college professor who came here a couple of years ago to teach at the university. She's a very smart lady, and next semester she will be lecturing at American University in D.C. She's never been to the East Coast, so Esther thought it would be nice if you two could meet, then she would have a local contact in the area once she arrives."

"What does she teach?"

"Philosophy and religion."

Jack scratched his head. "Great…well, I guess I would have a better chance if she were gay."

They quickly changed into their beach attire and hopped into Punjeeh's BMW. Within minutes they had passed through the Jaffa Gate and left the stone walls of the Old City behind, but it wasn't long before traffic stalled to a crawl. Jack saw that about a hundred yards ahead the road was blocked by barricades and armed soldiers. The sight of military personnel carrying machine guns on the city streets made him very uncomfortable. "What the hell is this?" he asked.

"An Israeli checkpoint. We're crossing into the occupied territory of the West Bank."

As they got closer, he could see they had detained a young Arab man. The soldiers saw the Israeli tags on Punjeeh's car and the medical sticker on the windshield and quickly waved them through.

"I wonder what that's all about," said Jack.

"He looks Palestinian," said Punjeeh. "He was probably trying to get through without a pass."

"A pass?"

"Yes. The West Bank has become a prison of sorts. Palestinians cannot enter Jerusalem without a pass from the Israeli government."

"Why?"

"Suicide bombers. The Israelis want to inspect all Palestinians coming out of the occupied territories to make sure they are not armed with explosives."

"It's too bad it's come to this," said Jack.

"It's madness, my friend, madness," said Punjeeh. "The irony of the situation is that we call this place the Holy Land."

Punjeeh's comment reminded Jack again of the change he had detected in his friend, the absence of any Catholic imagery in his home, and of the last phone conversation they had had when Punjeeh told him that being in the Holy Land had opened his eyes to some things. He decided that there was no better time than the present to ask about it.

"Punjeeh, you said something before about how living here had changed you, and you promised last night we could talk about it today. So I ask you again, what the hell is going on with you?"

Punjeeh looked over at Jack. "I was wondering when that question was coming," he said with a half smile.

Jack was silent, waiting for him to continue.

Punjeeh took a deep breath before beginning. "My friend, you know me as well as anyone. For years I was so sure of myself, I was so focused, I knew exactly what I wanted. I came from a good home, I married a nice girl, and I was well educated. Hell, I became a doctor, for God's sake. I wanted to help people. I moved here to begin a new job, we wanted to start a family, everything fit so perfectly into a neat little box."

"Sounds like a great life to me," said Jack.

"I thought so, too," replied Punjeeh. "And at the center of all this was my religion. I went to mass every Sunday, confession once a month, and I never missed a day of religious obligation. I was so excited to be in Jerusalem ... this so-called Holy Land."

Punjeeh paused, his face now grim.

"But after we arrived here and I began my new job in the ER, my perspective started to change. You see, Jack, I saw things at work, things that made me question what I had come to believe in all these years."

"What did you see?"

Punjeeh turned his head and looked Jack in the eye. "Death, Jack. I saw death. The death of young children, and the agony of their parents. And all so pointless. I saw Jewish children killed by suicide bombers and I saw Palestinian children killed by Israeli retaliatory strikes. It was horrific, absolute madness, all in the name of religion."

"Then about six months ago, a four-year-old girl was brought in with severe gunshot wounds to the neck and chest. She had been caught in the crossfire between Israeli solders and Palestinian rebels at a checkpoint, like the one we just passed."

"My God, that's terrible."

"Her mother was crying and screaming. They had to pull her away just so I could get a look at the little girl. I tried everything, Jack, but it was too late. There was nothing I could do." Punjeeh's eyes glazed over as he relived the scene in his mind. "No one knows whose side fired the fatal shot, but does it really matter?"

"I'm so sorry," Jack said, not knowing what else to say. "I don't know how you do it, seeing all that death. I couldn't do your job."

Punjeeh put his hand on Jack's and squeezed it tight. "I promise you, my friend, when a child dies in your arms, you'll never look at life the same again."

Jack felt a chill run down his spine.

"And for what?" Punjeeh asked out loud. "I wanted to know what on earth could make human beings inflict so much suffering on one another."

Jack could see the tears welling up in Punjeeh's eyes.

"And then it came to me, as clear as an unbridled moon," Punjeeh said and stopped.

"What was it?" Jack asked.

"Beliefs, Jack, beliefs. More specifically, religious beliefs. People kill each other here because they disagree with each other's religion, with each other's beliefs and ideas about God … in this place we call the Holy Land.

"And it was then that I decided I would not participate in the madness anymore. I wouldn't let any belief system rule my thinking, including that of my own religion. I will not participate in the 'I am right about God and you are not' madness ever again."

Jack was shaken by his friend's story, but was also afraid Punjeeh's traumatic experience might be clouding his vision. "I certainly understand why you would feel that way," he said cautiously. "But can you see that Christianity has nothing to do with the fight between the Muslims and Jews?"

Punjeeh sighed and shook his head. "The current controversy may not involve the Christians, but any superficial reading of history will provide numerous examples of bloody disagreements that do."

"But is that a good reason to give up on God?"

Punjeeh smiled. "My friend, I am sorry, I did not make myself clear. I have not given up on God; I've just given up on religion."

"Oh," said Jack, surprised by his friend's response. For some reason the thought that one could give up religion without giving up God hadn't occurred to him.

"It's not God that is causing this bloodshed," Punjeeh continued, "it's man."

"So that's the change I've detected in you these past few months?"

"I guess so," said Punjeeh. "I could tell in our conversations that you were becoming more interested in your Catholicism, and I'm very happy for you. At the same time, I don't share the enthusiasm that I would have a few years ago. But I can tell you that I am completely at peace with how I'm feeling. I don't know if it will last, but it's how I'm feeling right now."

Punjeeh's last statement helped put Jack's mind at ease. While he wasn't happy about his friend's change of heart, Jack was glad to see that Punjeeh was comfortable with it. And although he would never say it, Jack couldn't help but think that what had happened to Punjeeh was some kind of *crisis in faith*, and he hoped that his friend would return to their religion soon enough.

They continued driving silently for the next few moments. Jack refocused his attention on the surroundings and noticed that the farther they got from the checkpoint, the more the scenery changed. The clean, modern-looking city of Jerusalem had given way to run-down buildings and dusty streets.

"These living conditions seem to drop off pretty fast out here," Jack commented.

"It's a much tougher life on this side of the fence," Punjeeh replied, referring to the plight of the Palestinians. "Almost half of the inhabitants live below the poverty line, and a good job here pays no more than $100 per week."

"Whew," replied Jack, "that won't buy you lunch in D.C."

"It won't buy much more here either."

Jack was trying to imagine what it would be like to live on such meager wages when he spotted something unusual off in the distance. *Is that a brand new subdivision?* It looked like any one of a hundred upper-middle-class neighborhoods that he would see back home, but with one glaring addition. It was surrounded by a ten-foot-high barbed-wire fence and was guarded by armed soldiers. It reminded him of the checkpoint.

"What the heck is that?" Jack asked.

Punjeeh looked out the passenger window. "That, my friend, is a Jewish settlement. It's one of the things they are fighting about. The Jewish government seized this territory, called the West Bank, from the country of Jordan after their 1967 war. They began moving settlers in shortly thereafter. But the Palestinians hope that the West Bank will someday be part of an independent Palestine, so they are opposed to the settlements."

"Looks like pretty tight security. I wouldn't want to live there."

"Most of the Jews I know wouldn't either," Punjeeh replied, "but the settlers are primarily very orthodox Jews who believe that God promised them this land, and they are determined to keep it."

"God promised it to them?" Jack said with a look of skepticism.

"You see now what I mean about the trouble with beliefs?" Punjeeh asked with a faint smile.

⌒ᴍ⌒

# 9

*Present Day*

Punjeeh had mixed emotions as he sat in Chloe's office. While intensely intrigued by everything she and Professor King had said about the Gnostics, he was also troubled. "This is all fascinating," he exclaimed, "but quite the opposite of what I learned about the Gnostics in my church teachings. I was told that they were an early heretical movement which had been stamped out by the Catholic Church. Why have I never heard the things you've just told us before now?"

"Once the Literalists received the backing of the Roman Emperor," Chloe answered, "their hierarchy branded the Gnostics as heretics and destroyed almost all of their writings. For centuries, the only information we had about the Gnostics was from the treatises of the early Literalist church, written by priests called the Heresy Hunters."

Jack was amused. "You've got to be kidding," he said. "Heresy Hunters?"

"I'm afraid so," Professor King lamented. "And what they had to say about the Gnostics wasn't very complimentary, but since very few Gnostic writings had survived from antiquity, scholars had little ammunition with which to dispute the Heresy Hunters' claims."

"But fortunately, all of that changed some fifty years ago with the discovery of the *Gnostic Gospels*," Chloe added, "when several ancient Gnostic texts were discovered at Nag Hamadhi, Egypt, and they revolutionized our view of early Christianity. We knew such gospels existed because there are many negative references to them in the letters of the Heresy Hunters. But it was only after the discovery at Nag Hamadhi that we could read these gospels for ourselves, the most famous of which is the Gospel of Thomas. Not surprisingly, these works provided us with a very different view of the Gnostics from what had come to us from the Heresy Hunters and other Literalist priests."

Punjeeh's face illuminated immediately. "Of course," he exclaimed. "I've heard of the Gospel of Thomas. But I had no idea it was a Gnostic writing."

Jack acknowledged the same.

Chloe was glad they had found an outside reference point. "The Gospel of Thomas is in some ways very similar to the biblical gospels. In it, Jesus tells many of the same parables and teaches the same principles of love and forgiveness. In fact, many scholars think the Gospel of Thomas may be older than some of the biblical gospels because the parables and sayings of Jesus appear in Thomas in a more complete form."

She took a sip of coffee.

"But it also has one striking difference: it contains no historical or biographical information about Jesus. The virgin birth, the miracles he performed, the crucifixion … none of those stories are present in the Gospel of Thomas."

Her last statement puzzled Punjeeh. "Why do you think that is?"

"We can only assume that the author of the Gospel of Thomas, like most of the Gnostics, believed that the events of Jesus' life were of secondary importance to those of his teachings," Chloe answered. "This was, of course, the exact opposite of the Literalist church, which taught that belief in Jesus' act of dying on the cross for the sins of humanity was the paramount issue."

"That's very interesting," Jack said politely, while in truth he was becoming more suspicious of the Gnostics. Although he applauded their aspirations regarding gender equality – sexism was an issue he had always disapproved of in the Catholic Church – he was uncomfortable with some of the other Gnostic ideals; for instance, that Jehovah, the God of the Old Testament, was some type of false god.

Jack looked at Punjeeh, who he sensed was having the opposite reaction. "So what do you think of these Gnostics, Punj?"

"I wish they were still around," his friend answered, "then maybe I would go back to mass."

Chloe smiled. "Unfortunately for you and the Gnostics, the structure and simplicity of the Literalist church attracted many more followers than the Gnostic path."

"Unfortunately for mankind," Punjeeh replied solemnly, "most people need someone to lead them or something to lean on."

Jack was growing increasingly uncomfortable with the direction of the conversation, which he thought was bordering on anti-Catholic. He was tempted to point out that because this Gnostic style of Christianity had not survived to present day, it must have been inferior. But, he decided against it for the time being. Instead, he chose to steer their discussion back to the purpose of their meeting: deciphering the document. "What emperor is he referring to here?" he asked Chloe and pointed to the line in the paragraph which read, *The emperor claims a great vision of our Risen Lord and has become one of them.*

"He?" Chloe inquired.

"Yes," Jack answered quickly. "The author of the letter."

Chloe smiled. "What makes you think the author was a he?"

No sooner had she asked the question than Jack realized his blunder. "Or she," he offered timidly.

Punjeeh let out a chuckle. "She's got you on that one, my friend."

"Please remember that the Gnostics did not discriminate on the basis of sex," Chloe recounted, "so there's no necessary reason to think the author of this document was a man."

"Sorry," Jack said sheepishly, "just a figure of speech."

Chloe smiled. "I was just coming to that. The emperor here is undoubtedly the Roman Emperor Constantine, as he played a major role in the Gnostics' demise.

"You see, until 325 AD, Christianity was just one of many religions in a very culturally diverse Roman Empire. But when the Emperor Constantine converted to Christianity, the status of this relatively young religion was greatly elevated."

"When the king changes religions, his subjects generally follow suit," Professor King added, "and unfortunately for the Gnostics, Constantine converted to the Literalist form of Christianity."

Chloe nodded her head in agreement. "Many in the empire doubted if Constantine's conversion was spiritual as much as political, because the Literalist church, with its priests, bishops, and obedient followers, was the perfect vehicle to fulfill Constantine's goal of unifying the territories of Rome under one religion.

"But there were rumors throughout the empire that, secretly, Constantine still worshiped the gods of Greece and Rome…and these rumors may explain the next line of this document." She pointed to the sentence that read, *Oh what deception! If they only knew of Mithras, Dionysus, Adonis, and the many, many more.*

"Who are Mithras, Dino–?" Jack briefly attempted to pronounce the words.

"Those were a few of the Greek and Roman gods popular in the empire at that time," Professor King answered. "And I agree with Chloe, the author of this document probably thought that Constantine's conversion to Christianity was more political than spiritual. He was arguably the first Roman emperor to realize that it would be easier to control the vast Roman populace if they all adhered to one religion…and Christianity was a logical choice, because it had been experiencing rapid growth, had followers and churches throughout the empire, and the Literalist priests maintained substantial control over their followers.

"And, to consolidate his political base," the professor continued, "Constantine called the Council of Nicaea in 325 AD, which was a meeting of bishops from the Literalist Christian churches throughout the empire. His ultimate aim was to unify them all into one 'universal' church."

"Universal," said Punjeeh thoughtfully, "the meaning of the Latin word for catholic."

"Exactly," Chloe confirmed. "It was after the Council of Nicaea that the Literalist church officially became the Roman Catholic Church… and for his role in the process, Constantine was recognized as the Holy Roman Emperor. From that moment on, the Catholic pope, aka the Bishop of Rome, was now under the protection of the emperor's armies…and in return, the emperor of Rome had the loyalty and following of the growing Christian faithful."

"*The unification of church and state is complete,*" said Punjeeh, referring to another line of the translated scroll.

"Quite right, Dr. Punjeeh," nodded Professor King. "Politicians have often used religion as a tool, and with all the various religions active throughout the Roman Empire at the time, it's not hard to imagine the appeal that uniting under one religion would have to someone in Constantine's position."

Punjeeh's expression turned ominous. "Given the state of affairs in the Holy Land today, Professor King, one religion doesn't sound like a bad idea now either."

"Perhaps so, Dr. Punjeeh, perhaps so."

"So is that what is meant by this next line?" Jack asked, looking at Chloe. He pointed to the line that read, *His council at Nicaea has decreed their ignorance.*

"Perhaps," she answered and paused for a moment, "but the use of the word *decreed* makes me think of the famous Nicene Creed, adopted by the council in 325, which amounted to a core statement of beliefs from the now universal, or catholic, church."

"The Apostles' Creed," said Punjeeh.

Jack was familiar with the Apostles' Creed. "Sure, we recite it in every mass."

"That's right," answered Chloe.

Jack tried to remember the wording. *We believe in one God, the father the almighty, maker of heaven and earth ...* He couldn't remember the rest, but he had never noticed anything objectionable when reading it in church. "So what's so ignorant about it?"

"Well, the first version of the Apostles' Creed, the one authored by the Council at Nicaea, has been modified slightly over the centuries. So let's take a look at the original and see."

Chloe turned around in her chair and scanned the books against the back wall. "Here we are," she said as she stood up and took a large book from the top shelf. She flipped through the pages until she found what she wanted and then laid the open book on the desk facing Jack and Punjeeh.

"This is a translation of the Nicene Creed as it was written in 325." She sat down, pointing to the indented passage on the page.

> We believe in one God the Father Almighty, Maker of all things visible and invisible; and in *one Lord Jesus Christ, the only begotten of the Father, that is, of the substance of the Father*, God of God, light of light, true God of true God, begotten not made, *of the same substance with the Father* through whom all things were made both in heaven and on earth; who for us men and

our salvation descended, was incarnate, and was made man, suffered and rose again the third day, ascended into heaven and cometh to judge the living and the dead. *Those who say: There was a time when He was not, and He was not before He was begotten; and that He was made out of nothing or who maintain that He is of another hypostasis or another substance than the Father, or that the Son of God is created, or mutable, or subject to change, them the Catholic Church anathematizes.*

Jack and Punjeeh read it over. "What does *anathematize* mean?" asked Jack.

"To damn to hell," said Punjeeh ominously. "Those who do not believe as they do, the Roman Catholic Church damns to hell."

"Ouch," said Jack with a look of disbelief. "I don't think that's in the one we recite."

"I think it's safe to say that the Catholic Church has changed for the better since then," said Chloe lightheartedly. "That part has been removed. But the anathematization was aimed at something specific. Take a look again at the italicized sections of the creed."

Jack and Punjeeh reread them.

"They all reference the belief that Jesus and God are one and the same," said Punjeeh.

"That's right," said Chloe. "The Catholic Church condemned anyone who didn't believe that Jesus and God—and by God they meant Jehovah from the Old Testament—were one and the same. And you do remember what I said about the Gnostics' opinion of Jehovah, right?"

"Is that the part where they said God was a narcissistic egomaniac?" Jack quipped.

"Something like that," Chloe replied with a twinkle in her eye. "While the Gnostics might equate Jesus with whom they considered was the 'real' God, or The One Life, they certainly didn't believe that Jesus was the same as Jehovah. So much of the Nicene Creed is aimed specifically at refuting Gnostic principles."

"And the decree of the council was the beginning of the end for the Gnostics," Professor King spoke up, "after which, they had very, very few good days."

Chloe again nodded her head in agreement. "With the Literalist

Christians united and receiving the backing of imperial Rome, the next several years proved to be horrendous for the Gnostics. They were branded as heretics, their writings were burned, and their teachers tortured and killed. Their existence was practically erased from history."

Punjeeh looked over at Jack. "And you wonder why I've lost faith in religion?"

Jack didn't respond.

"And, there is more evidence that Constantine's conversion was primarily for political gain," Chloe added, "as it was under his direction that the Catholic Church assimilated many traditions of the existing Greek and Roman religions into Christianity, presumably to make it easier for other non-Christians to convert, too."

Her comment made Jack uneasy. "*Assimilated traditions*? What do you mean?"

"For example, the birth of Mithras, one of the Roman gods mentioned in this letter, had been celebrated for centuries on December 25, the day after the winter solstice, or the shortest day of the year. The ancients viewed December 25 as the birthday of the sun, and since Mithras was the god of light, they thought it was only natural that his birth should be celebrated on that day, or the first day of the new sun. But when Constantine converted to Christianity, he decreed that Jesus' birthday would also be celebrated on December 25."

"The birth of the sun," added Professor King, "became the birth of the son."

"You've got to be kidding," said Jack with a look of disbelief.

"No," Chloe smiled, "this is, in fact, fairly common knowledge."

Jack looked to Punjeeh for confirmation. "She's right, Jack," he answered. "The church celebrates the birth of Jesus on December 25, but admits that there is no historical reason for doing so." Punjeeh paused and then winked at him. "But it is a 1 in 365 chance."

"Very funny," said Jack.

Punjeeh returned their attention to the translation, as there was a line he had been curious about since the beginning. "What on earth does this mean?" he asked, pointing to the line that read, *What we have started they have overtaken.*

"As you mentioned earlier," Chloe answered, "the Catholic Church theology states that the Literalists were the first Christians, and that Gnosticism was a later heretical development. I know this may sound very strange, but the Gnostics claimed that the *opposite* was true. They asserted that they were, in fact, the original Christians, or the true keepers of Jesus' teachings, and that it was Literalism and Catholicism that developed afterward."

"You can't be serious," Jack retorted immediately.

"I'm afraid it's true," added Professor King. "The Gnostics claimed that they were the first Christians, and that St. Paul and the authors of the biblical gospels were all Gnostics."

Despite his self-admitted ignorance concerning the history of the Bible and the early Christian church, Jack's personal convictions urged him to defend the faith of his upbringing. "That just can't be," he objected again. "This whole discussion is starting to sound like an ideological fantasy."

Professor King exhaled deeply. "As an ordained Christian minister, I can understand your objection, Jack," he offered sympathetically. "But, as an academic, I must say it is a hypothesis worthy of investigation."

Punjeeh was more objective. "Is there any evidence to support the claim that the Gnostics were the first Christians?"

Chloe was the first to reply. "I think it ultimately boils down to how you interpret the gospels. The Literalists said they were infallible historical documents and that belief in their infallibility was the key to salvation. The Gnostics said something entirely different. They saw the biblical gospels as primarily allegorical, and belief in them as only the first step on the path to gnosis. They taught that Jesus entrusted his closest disciples with additional information, what they also called *the secret mysteries*."

"Like the secret mysteries mentioned in the letter—" Punjeeh exclaimed, pointing to the last paragraph of the translation.

"Precisely," said Chloe, smiling. "Unlike the Literalists, the Gnostics taught that believing the gospels to be a historical account of the life of Jesus Christ was the first step in becoming a Christian, but that the *secret mysteries* were revealed to the Gnostic adherent later, as he or she progressed toward *experiencing* or *knowing* God. In short, the Gnostics saw the Literalists as Christians who never got past the basics."

Punjeeh's fascination grew. "That's amazing. What were some of these secret mysteries?"

"Unfortunately no one knows for sure," Professor King answered despairingly. "The Gnostics claimed that the mysteries were not to be written down, but only passed verbally from teacher to student... but there is an early church legend that states that the First Secret Mystery of the Gnostics had something to say about Jesus' crucifixion and resurrection."

Jack and Punjeeh were silent for a moment.

"Let me guess, these Gnostics didn't believe that Jesus was raised from the dead," Jack said with disdain.

"We really don't know," Professor King answered. "But one thing is certain: the Gnostics claimed to have some secret knowledge about the crucifixion and resurrection of Jesus, and it is also clear from the writings of the Heresy Hunters that the Literalist church was very concerned about it. They did not want this information shared."

"And that's what makes the last line of this scroll so intriguing," said Chloe, pointing to the translation: *I will record the First Secret Mystery of Jesus and hide it in the caves of our forefathers. Let God keep it safe from destruction, and ordain whoever finds it, so that the truth and the mystery shall someday be reborn.*

"To me, it sounds like the author of this letter must have written the First Secret Mystery down, perhaps on another scroll," Chloe explained. "But where that writing is now, it's impossible to know."

Jack and Punjeeh exchanged glances. Again, they were reading each other's minds.

"Actually," Jack said a little cautiously, "I might know."

✳

# 10

*1 Day Earlier–Afternoon*

Caleb got out of school and headed for the antique shop. Youseff was absent that day, and his younger sister had informed the class that he wasn't feeling well. As Caleb suspected, the proprietor was in his usual place, sitting in the rocking chair on the shop's front porch.

"Good afternoon, lad," the old man said as Caleb approached.

"Hello, sir."

"Where's your friend?"

"He's home sick today, but it probably worked out for the better. I wanted to talk to you alone."

The old man appreciated his directness. "I'm listening," he said, leaning forward in his rocking chair.

"Let's say we did find a couple of scrolls in that jar yesterday."

"A couple?" the man interrupted. "That's fantastic. I figured you had found one, but two?"

Caleb was surprised. "How did you know?"

"Young man, I'm seventy-five years old. I know how to listen to every word that isn't spoken."

Caleb hedged. "Well, I'm not saying we found any scrolls, but let's just say for a moment that we did find two, and we wanted you to sell them for us in one of those quiet sales. How much could we get for them?"

"Caleb," he said assuringly, "you can trust me. I am not going to tell anyone you found the scrolls, regardless of whether we do business or not. I wouldn't have lasted this many years here if I didn't know how to keep a secret."

Caleb let out his breath in relief. "Okay," he said.

"But I do have a confession to make. I had a feeling after you left the other day that you had found a scroll, so I called another collector friend of mine and asked if he knew of any parties who would be interested in acquiring a Dead Sea scroll, but I made no mention of you or Youseff, I can assure you."

"And what did he say?"

"Well, depending on the condition, he said an authentic Dead Sea scroll could bring as much as one thousand dollars U.S."

Caleb was aghast. "One thousand dollars?"

"Each, in this case," the old man added.

Caleb couldn't believe his ears. Two thousand dollars exponentially exceeded the ten or twenty dollars he had planned on asking at one of the tourist areas. But his excitement was soon followed by fear. "But what if the Israelis find out? Something that valuable, they'll lock us up and we'll never be seen again."

"They won't find out," the old man said. "And even if they do, your identity will be a secret to everyone but me, so they could never trace the scrolls back to either of you."

"And what do you get out of it?" Caleb asked.

"My fee will be paid by the purchaser," the old man replied. "You don't need to trouble yourself with that."

"Okay," Caleb replied. "Where do we go from here?"

"I need to see the scrolls," the old man replied. "I need to make sure they are what we think they are, and then I will call my friend to set up the transaction."

"Give me fifteen minutes," Caleb replied as he hurried out the door.

⌒≈⌒

# II

As they continued driving east toward the Dead Sea the signs of civilization became sparse and the land more arid. The taller trees disappeared, giving way to squatty scrub brush that dotted the rolling hills.

"We've entered the Judean Desert," Punjeeh replied, "where Jesus is believed to have spent his forty days and forty nights in solitude. And just on the other side of that is the Dead Sea. We're going to the town of El-Amin. It's really just a hotel and a small market, but it has a public beach that's usually not too crowded this time of year. It's a favorite spot of the local Jewish inhabitants."

When they arrived in El-Amin, Jack was struck by how small the place actually was. There was the beach, a row of gift shops, and a large building that looked like a hotel. "You weren't kidding," he said. "There's not much here."

"Yes, but the water is great, and I don't like the crowds at the larger places."

Punjeeh parked the car and they headed toward the beach. It was fairly deserted, with only a handful of sunbathers strewn along the sandy shore.

"I'll race you," said Jack as he broke off into a sprint for the water. Punjeeh didn't increase his pace at all.

As Jack hit the water at a gallop, some of the waves splashed up onto his tongue. The resulting taste stopped him in his tracks.

"Yuck!" He turned back to Punjeeh, who had just reached the edge of the shore. "That is the saltiest water I've ever tasted."

"My friend, the salt content is so high that nothing can live in it. That's why it's called the Dead Sea."

Jack shot Punjeeh a look. "Didn't you say its waters were supposed to be healing?" he asked sarcastically.

"That's right. Taking a brief swim in this water is excellent for your skin and is a great stress reliever ... but you're not supposed to drink it!" he said with a grin.

"Watch!" Punjeeh ordered as he walked in up to his waist, held up his arms, and then fell backwards into the water. Instead of sinking, his body seemed to levitate at the surface. He looked like a fishing cork bobbing along in the sun. "You try it."

Jack was baffled by what he'd just seen. He inched his way into the water, and as it got deeper, he felt the strangest sensation. It was as if the water were pushing on him, holding him up. "What's going on?" he asked as he made his way toward Punjeeh.

"Lie back," Punjeeh commanded.

He followed Punjeeh's instructions, and as he did, he imagined he was riding on a magic carpet. The water just picked him up and held him there.

"Wow," Jack said, as he hung in suspension.

"It's the salt. The water is so dense with it that the human body becomes extremely buoyant," Punjeeh said with a grin. "It's almost impossible to drown here ... but please don't try to prove me wrong."

They continued their floating experience for the next half hour or so until the doctor in Punjeeh spoke up again. "We better get out. Too much exposure to this water can be harmful."

As they exited and began drying off, Jack noticed a young Arab boy about high-school age approaching various sunbathers. He was carrying a brown paper bag and was attempting to show its contents to whoever would listen. To his dismay, most were waving him off as soon as he addressed them.

Jack always had a soft spot for salespeople, mainly because he knew well the difficulties of cold calling. "Looks like we'll be next," he said to Punjeeh as he pointed out the young boy who was working his way toward them.

Punjeeh looked over and saw the youngster approaching. "I wouldn't recommend buying anything here," Punjeeh replied quickly. "The unlicensed street vendors are just like the watch salesmen in New York and D.C., selling cheap replicas that last for about a week. Esther knows a handful of respectable curio shops where you can buy quality souvenirs at very reasonable prices. "

Jack just smiled. He remembered what a bargain hunter Punjeeh was.

"Are you Americans?" the young man asked Jack, while looking dubiously at Punjeeh, as if he was trying to surmise his ethnicity. Punjeeh returned the uneasy glance, reiterating his dislike of street vendors.

Jack sensed his dilemma. "Yes, we're Americans," he responded with a chuckle, looking over at Punjeeh, who just rolled his eyes.

"I have something very old and valuable to show you."

The boy reached into his bag and produced two old scrolls.

"These are ancient writings. They were found in the desert not far from here and would make an excellent memento of your trip to Palestine."

Punjeeh shook his head. "You see, Jack, what did I tell you? I'm sure they're priceless," he said sarcastically.

Jack didn't pay any attention. "May I see them?" he asked.

"Yes, sir."

The boy handed Jack the two scrolls. The paper certainly looked ancient. He unrolled one slightly to reveal some of the writing.

"Okay, how much?"

"Only ten dollars each," the boy replied enthusiastically.

Jack was surprised he hadn't asked for more. Then he remembered what Punjeeh had told him about the living conditions in the West Bank. "Okay," he said, "I'll take..."

Before Jack could finish his sentence he was interrupted by a boisterous female voice calling from a few yards away. "Excuse me. Young man, I've changed my mind. I'd like to buy one of your items."

Jack looked up to see a heavy-set, middle-aged woman in a black one-piece bathing suit rumbling down the beach toward them. He noticed that one of her legs had been amputated just below the knee, and she wore a prosthesis, a curved metal railing about three inches wide that extended from the knee and turned at where her ankle once was, forming what looked like a shortened snow ski in place of a foot. Jack was amazed at how quickly she moved around with it. "I say I changed my mind," the woman said in a distinctly American accent.

"Do you still have one available? What was your best price again? Five dollars?"

The boy's excitement evaporated. He looked back at Jack, now very uncomfortable. As the woman reached the group, she sensed the awkward feeling in the air. "Oh, has this gentlemen already agreed to purchase them?"

The boy didn't say anything, but looked at Jack to answer the question.

"Yes," Jack said. "But on second thought, I'll just buy one. You can have the other one." He handed her one of the scrolls.

"Oh, you must be American," she said upon hearing Jack speak. "Isn't this place fascinating?"

"It's magnificent," Jack replied.

She took the scroll. "We've had a wonderful time. I'm here with a church tour group. I can't believe it's been two and a half weeks already. But it's back to Baltimore in a couple of days."

"Baltimore?" Jack asked. "I live in Virginia, right near D.C. I just arrived last night. I'm here visiting my old college roommate." He gestured to Punjeeh.

"Hello," Punjeeh said.

"Oh, you live here?" she asked. "That must be fascinating. What brought you here, your job?"

"Yes," Punjeeh replied. "And my wife's family is here. I'm an emergency room doctor."

"Oh, how admirable." She held up one of the scrolls. "Now I've got something else to show my eighth-grade students when I get back home. Thanks very much, young man ... and it was nice meeting you both." She handed the boy five one-dollar bills before turning around and heading for the hotel.

The boy eyed Jack hesitantly. "Would you still like to buy one, sir? The price is only five dollars."

Jack reached into his pants pocket and pulled out his money clip. He removed a ten-dollar bill and handed it to the boy. "No, a deal is a deal."

The boy's eyes lit up as he reached for the bill. "Thank you, sir." He quickly turned around and ran off toward the mainland.

"That was very kind of you, my friend," Punjeeh said. "I see you haven't lost your charitable spirit."

Jack chuckled. "Hold on to the accolades for a moment. I have a selfish motive too."

"And what's that?"

Jack unrolled the scroll again to expose the writing to Punjeeh. "I think this writing is Greek ... and didn't you say Esther's friend was from Greece?"

Punjeeh laughed. "That's my Jack, always creating an opportunity."

# 12

Caleb was filled with anticipation as he arrived at the old tree where they had hidden the scrolls. Palms sweating, he reached inside the hole to retrieve his booty.

Nothing.

Frantically, he moved his hand around the hollowed-out trunk while becoming more alarmed with each passing second.

He collapsed to his knees and buried his face in his hands. He couldn't believe they weren't there. *Where could they be?* Suddenly he remembered that Youseff had been absent from school that day.

Infuriated, he broke into a desperate run toward Youseff's house. As he got closer he saw a smiling Youseff waving to him from the front steps.

Caleb ran up to his face, yelling, "Where the hell are they?"

Youseff's smile changed to a perplexed expression. "Where's what?"

"The scrolls, you idiot," Caleb shouted. "What did you do with them?"

"I didn't do anything with them," Youseff said, angrily. "We left them in the tree, remember?"

"Of course I remember. But I just went to get them and they weren't there. Where are they?"

"I don't know! I told you I didn't do anything with them!"

"Well, if you didn't then who did? Because they aren't where we left them!" Caleb screamed.

Youseff looked at him blankly. Then his expression changed to horror. "Tariq!" he shouted with disgust.

"What?" Caleb stammered.

Youseff looked fearfully at Caleb. "I'm sorry, Caleb. I told Tariq about the scrolls…but he promised not to say anything!"

Caleb was stupefied. "I can't believe you!" he scolded. "And you told him where they were?"

Youseff was almost too afraid to answer. "Yes," he said sheepishly.

"You're an idiot!" Caleb yelled. "Come on, we've got to find him."

# 13

When Jack and Punjeeh returned from their excursion to the Dead Sea, Esther met them at the front door.

"Jack!" Esther shouted as he and Punjeeh walked in. She came over and hugged him. Fair-skinned, buxom, and slightly taller than Jack, she liked to wear her auburn hair bobbed, and today was no exception.

"I'm so happy you're here!" Esther exclaimed. "Thank you for coming all this way!"

"My pleasure," he responded jubilantly. "It was my first chance to take a break and I couldn't imagine going anyplace else. And I can see you're taking good care of my ole pal here." He gestured toward Punjeeh's belly, which Jack noticed when they were swimming was a tad larger than in their college days.

"He makes it easy on me," she said. "Whatever I put in front of him, he eats."

Jack had always admired Esther and Punjeeh's relationship. Some of his other college friends had married, and that was the last he ever saw of them. But it wasn't that way with her. She and Punjeeh maintained their independence, both keeping active lives apart from each other. It wasn't that they weren't a close couple; quite the contrary. She said the autonomy made them enjoy their time together even more. Jack mentioned to Esther once that he admired that aspect of her and Punjeeh's relationship and she quipped back to him, "I said 'til death do us part, not breakfast, lunch, and dinner."

She welcomed Punjeeh with a kiss. "I missed you."

"I missed you too," he replied bashfully. Punjeeh had always been uncomfortable with public affection.

"I'm glad some things haven't changed," Jack blurted out.

Esther smiled and shot Jack an understanding glance. "No, he's the same old Punjeeh. He's just loosened up a bit."

The doorbell rang.

"Oh, Chloe must be here," Esther said. She opened the front door. "Chloe, come in, please."

Esther gave her a welcoming hug as she walked in. Jack was pleasantly surprised. Punjeeh had said she was attractive, but in the nice sort of general way in which Punjeeh referred to a lot of people. And besides, Jack wondered, how attractive could a college professor be?

Very, apparently.

"Hi, Punjeeh," Chloe said warmly.

"Hello, Chloe." Punjeeh stuck out his hand to greet her. "And please, allow me to introduce you to my friend, Jack." He gestured to Jack. "Jack Stanton, Chloe Eisenberg."

Jack extended his hand and flashed his trademark smile, "It's a pleasure to meet you."

"Likewise," Chloe said politely.

"They walked in the door just before you got here, Chloe," said Esther. "I've got dinner on the table."

They congregated at the round dining room table where Esther had place settings for four. "I hope you like hummus, Jack."

Jack gawked at the pasty dish in front of him. "Me, too," he said and laughed. "What is it?"

"Don't worry, Jack," Punjeeh said, "Esther makes the best hummus in all of Jerusalem."

"I can vouch for that," Chloe concurred.

Jack soon learned that hummus is a popular Mediterranean dish usually made with ground chickpeas and an assortment of oils and spices, and eaten with bread or crackers. He thought it looked like bean dip.

"So tell me, Jack, how was your first day in Israel?" Esther asked as Punjeeh dove into the hummus.

"Unbelievable," he said. "In the morning, I went down to Via Dolorosa."

"Did you go inside the Church of the Holy Sepulchre?" Esther asked.

"Yes, it was awesome. And I'd like to go to a mass there before I leave. Is that where you go to mass, Punjeeh?"

Punjeeh paused from the hummus. "I'm afraid I haven't been to mass in a few months," he said slyly. "But I'll be happy to go with you if you'd like me to."

Jack snickered good-naturedly and then turned to Chloe. "You know, Chloe, the irony here is that when we were in college I never went to church, and Punjeeh never missed. And now that I find myself wanting to get more into it, he doesn't want to go anymore."

The group chuckled at Jack's remark, but Chloe showed a keener interest. "I'm curious, what makes you want to 'get more into it,' as you said?"

Jack paused briefly before answering. "I'm not sure," he said. "A combination of things, really, or maybe it's just because I'm getting older," he said with a grin. "But I've been feeling a bit unfulfilled lately. I mean, I've spent a lot of time at work, and, well, probably too much time at work."

"And what do you do?" she asked.

"I work in the financial markets," he replied, "advising people on stocks, bonds, and other investments."

"And he's very good at it, too," Esther added.

Punjeeh jumped in. "That's right, Chloe, he's quite the prognosticator. He boldly forecast the American tech stock collapse of a few years ago...and when the bottom fell out, all the newspapers crowned him the new king of financial soothsaying."

A part of Jack was embarrassed by Punjeeh's accolade, but another part of him wanted to high-five him under the table. "I got lucky," he said with pretend modesty.

Chloe picked up the pretense. "That's impressive," she said. "I've considered purchasing stocks before, but I must admit I find the prospect quite intimidating."

"Me, too," Esther added. "How do you know whether a stock is a good buy or not, Jack?"

"In many ways it's much simpler than you think," he replied casually, relishing the opportunity to demonstrate his business prowess in front of Chloe. "You've got to look at the fundamentals of the company and ask some basic questions. For instance, what are the company's assets and liabilities? Does the business have a good management team? What's the growth potential for the industry? I like to examine the core components of a company and determine its fair value even before looking at the stock price."

"So you're predicting what you think the price of the stock should be?" Punjeeh asked for clarification.

"Yes. I estimate the value of the entire company, and then divide that by the number of shares they've issued to determine the stock's fair price. For example, if I think a company is worth ten million dollars, and they have ten million shares outstanding, then the stock price on the open market should be one dollar each."

Chloe was intrigued. "And how often is the actual share price consistent with what you think it should be?"

"Almost never," Jack replied with a chuckle. "But that's when it gets interesting.

"I would say that ninety-nine percent of the time the price per share is more than I think it should be. Consequently, I don't buy them. But then there's that one percent of companies whose stock is priced below my estimation of fair value, and therefore the most likely ones to go up in price ... and I buy all I can."

Punjeeh shook his head and sighed. "Oh, Jack, you make it sound too easy."

"You could do it," Jack assured him. "But you have to do your homework."

"How can you be sure a company is worth what you think it is?" Esther asked.

"I'm never entirely sure," he replied. "It's really just my best guess. And ultimately that's all it is for anybody, because stock certificates are just pieces of paper. They are only worth what people believe they are worth."

"Thanks for the lesson," Chloe spoke up. "But I think I had better leave the stock picking to the professionals."

They continued eating and made light conversation, comparing life in Israel and the United States, their careers, and the latest books they had read.

As they were finishing dinner, Esther said, "Jack, my friend Chloe here will be coming to D.C. to teach for a semester. She'll be a visiting professor at American University."

"That's great," said Jack. "D.C. is a fascinating place."

Chloe smiled. "I've been to the United States only once, and that was to Miami."

"Well, D.C. is quite different from south Florida, nowhere near as colorful and a lot colder in the wintertime. I live in the D.C. area, in northern Virginia. I'd be happy to show you around or help in any way I can."

"That's a very kind offer," Chloe replied politely.

"So what subjects will you be teaching while you're there?" Jack asked.

"Philosophy and religion," she replied. "My specialty is ancient Greece."

"Oh, that's right," Jack feigned surprise. "Punjeeh mentioned you were originally from Greece. So do you speak Greek?"

"Yes," said Chloe, looking at Jack like she was wondering where he was going with the question. "Do you?"

"Oh no, no," said Jack, smiling and shaking his head. "It's just that I bought a souvenir from a kid at the beach today and I think the writing is in Greek. Could you look at it and tell me what it says?"

"I'll give it a try," Chloe replied.

"It's still in the car, Jack. I'll go down and get it for you," Punjeeh offered.

"That's okay, I'll get it."

Jack got up from the table and was heading to the door when he heard Esther ask, "So how do you think Ben will handle you being gone for so long?"

*Ben?* Jack thought to himself as he slowed down to hear her answer.

"It won't be easy," Chloe replied. "And I don't know whom it will be harder on, him or me."

Jack couldn't help but be discouraged at the news that Chloe had a boyfriend. But he certainly wasn't surprised. She was attractive, smart, and also had some mysterious quality that he couldn't quite label. This only added to her appeal.

Jack quickly retrieved the scroll from the car and returned to the house. He unrolled the document and placed it on the table in front of her. "Is this writing in Greek?"

Chloe studied it for a moment and then ruffled her brow. She ran her fingers over the exposed paper to feel its texture. She looked up at Jack and with a deadly serious tone asked, "Where did you get this?"

Jack was taken back by the interrogation. Punjeeh and Esther were also struck by the change in Chloe's demeanor "Uh…I bought it off some kid at the beach today," Jack answered cautiously.

"What beach?" she demanded as she looked over at Punjeeh, hoping for a more complete explanation.

"At El-Amin," Punjeeh said. "On the Dead Sea."

Chloe eyes grew wider as she raised her head back, like she couldn't believe her ears.

"Oh my gosh!" Esther exclaimed when she realized what Chloe was thinking.

Jack and Punjeeh glanced blankly at each other and then at the ladies, still without a clue as to what they were referencing.

"Hello, Punjeeh," Chloe said incredulously. "You bought an old scroll on the banks of the Dead Sea. Does that ring any bells?"

Punjeeh squinted in thought for a moment before an epiphanic expression washed over his face, "Of course, the Dead Sea Scrolls! But you don't think that this could be one of them, do you?"

Chloe rubbed the corner of the scroll with her thumb and index finger. "Well, I couldn't say for sure, but based on the texture of this parchment, it's obviously a very, very old document. No one would go to this much trouble for a fake."

"I remember hearing something about these Dead Sea Scrolls before," Jack recollected, "but what exactly are they?"

"More than 900 ancient scroll fragments were found in caves along the coast of the Dead Sea in the mid-twentieth century," Chloe answered. "They were a collection of religious writings from a monastic community of Jews called the Essenes."

"Wouldn't that be fascinating, Jack," Esther exclaimed, "you purchasing a Dead Sea Scroll."

"Let's not jump to conclusions just yet," Chloe warned. "I think you have something very old here, but I won't know until I examine it more closely. It may not be a traditional Dead Sea Scroll."

Punjeeh was still embarrassed that he did not remember a connection between the Dead Sea and ancient scrolls earlier. "I feel so foolish," he said, looking at the scroll on the table. "This could be an amazing find."

Jack gazed at the strange lettering on the brittle page in front of him. "So can you tell us what it says?"

"That's going to take a little time," Chloe said. "This isn't just Greek, it's Ancient Greek. I'm going to have to pull out the books for this one. If it's okay with you, I'd like to take it over to my office and begin translation immediately."

Jack hesitated. Although impressed by Chloe's knowledge and credentials, the businessman in him was uncomfortable leaving a possible treasure like this in the care of a stranger. He looked over at Punjeeh, who gave him a slight nod.

"Okay," Jack said nervously. "But how long before you'll have it translated?"

"I'm going over right now. With any luck, I'll call you in the morning."

# 14

Jack hardly slept as he eagerly awaited Chloe's report. The previous day's events had made his head spin. He had visited the place where Christ was crucified, floated like a cork in the Dead Sea, and, by luck, acquired an old scroll of potentially incredible value. He could only wonder what today would bring.

Fortunately, he didn't have to wait long.

He and Punjeeh were having breakfast when the phone rang.

"Good morning," Punjeeh answered.

"Hi, Punjeeh, it's Chloe. Is Jack available?"

"Yes. Just a minute," he said, handing the phone to Jack.

Jack grabbed the phone. "Hey, Chloe. What's up?" he asked anxiously.

"I've completed the translation."

"Great…so do we have one of those Dead Sea Scrolls?"

"No, definitely not—"

Jack grimaced. This was not the answer he was hoping for. "Damn! Well, what is it then?"

"I think it may be something far more interesting," she replied.

"What do you mean?" Jack's eyes flared with excitement again.

"It would be easier to go over it with you in person. Can you come to my office this morning?"

"Hold on a minute," Jack replied. He turned to Punjeeh. "How soon before we can be at Chloe's office?"

"Fifteen minutes."

Chloe heard Punjeeh's answer in the background. "Great, I'll explain then. And one more thing, Jack, I'd like to have one of my colleagues in the religion department join us, Professor Artemus King, as he may be able to help us decipher its meaning. Would that be okay with you?"

"Sure, whatever you think is best. See you then."

Punjeeh had been trying to guess the content of the conversation by Jack's changing expressions. "What did she say?" he asked as soon as Jack hung up.

"She said it wasn't a Dead Sea Scroll," Jack said, looking perplexed. "But that it may be something better ... whatever that means."

Punjeeh was also mystified by her ambiguity. "Well, I know Chloe, and she doesn't mince words. I can't wait to find out what it is."

# 15

Professor King and Chloe listened to Jack in astonishment as he gave them the full account of their day at the beach, and how he had held another scroll in his hand before willingly passing it to the middle-school teacher from Baltimore.

Finally, Professor King asked the question that was on everyone's mind. "Can you get it back?" he asked.

"I don't know," Jack said ruefully. "We can try. She looked like she was staying at the hotel on the beach. It won't hurt to go back there and ask."

"Gentlemen, I would very much like to see that other scroll. And I can say unequivocally that if the scroll you have here, not to mention the other, proves authentic pending further scientific evaluation, the college would be very interested in purchasing them both."

Professor King's comment was music to Jack's ears, but the possibility of the scroll having value raised other concerns. "Are there any legal issues we should be aware of regarding a find like this?" he asked. "I mean, will the government have a claim?"

"I don't see an issue here right now," Professor King replied. "You purchased the scroll in a perfectly legitimate manner. And since I haven't heard of anyone reporting items such as these as stolen, we can presume that the person who sold them was authorized to do so. Of course he obviously didn't know what he had, or he'd have sold them for far more.

"The next issue would be how this person came into possession of these items. Chances are they were discovered somewhere nearby, certainly in the West Bank, as it is highly unlikely that someone from outside of the occupied territory would have traveled all the way to the small beach at El-Amin to sell them. If this presumption is correct, then the Jewish government would face a political maelstrom if it tried to claim something that was discovered on Palestinian soil."

"What about the Palestinian government?" Punjeeh asked.

"Since the writings are not Islamic, I doubt they'd be bothered by it, either," the Professor continued. "There have been many ancient items unearthed over the years in the West Bank that had religious significance to Christians, and the Palestinian government's position has been to stay out of such matters."

"I agree with Professor King," Chloe added. "I doubt anyone would travel from outside the West Bank to sell something like this at El-Amin. In addition, the scroll itself gives us a clue as to where its author intended to hide it: *in the caves of our forefathers.*"

Jack and Punjeeh exchanged bewildered looks.

"The Essenes I mentioned last night," she continued, "those who wrote the Dead Sea Scrolls, inhabited the caves around the Dead Sea, and they are considered by many scholars to be the Jews that became the first Christians, whom the Gnostics considered their forefathers."

"That's right," Professor King concurred. "The Essenes were one of the three sects of Judaism that were active some two-thousand years ago, and undoubtedly the Jews who converted to Christianity. The other two branches were the Pharisees and the Sadducees, whom you may remember from the New Testament."

Jack thought for a moment. "The Pharisees and the Sadducees... they were the ones that crucified Jesus, right?" he asked, trying to sound knowledgeable when in fact he was repeating something the tour guide had said the previous day.

"According to the New Testament, yes," replied Chloe. "And while the New Testament gospels are highly critical of the Pharisees and the Sadducees, they never mention the Essenes. Consequently, some scholars interpret this silence as evidence that the first Christians were Essene converts, which I think is quite plausible when you examine the similarities between the Essenes and the early Christians."

"Really?" asked Punjeeh, somewhat surprised he had never heard this before. "What types of similarities?"

"For one," she answered, "the Essenes were strongly Messianic;

they believed that the Messiah would come to save the world in their lifetime."

"But I thought most Jews held strong Messianic beliefs in those days," Punjeeh reasoned.

"That's correct," Chloe confirmed, "many Jews in antiquity were anxiously awaiting the Messiah, but most expected him to be a great warrior or king, one who would dispel the Romans by means of violence. That's where the Essenes were different. They believed that the Messiah may not come as a warrior, but as a spiritual teacher or rabbi instead."

"Oh ... ," Jack said, suddenly realizing what she was getting at. "You mean someone more like Jesus."

"That's right," she replied. "Based on the theological beliefs articulated in the Dead Sea Scrolls, it appears that the Essenes would have been uniquely open to the idea that a spiritual teacher, or someone like Jesus, could be the Messiah."

"And there were other similarities between the Essenes and the early Christians," Chloe continued, "the most striking of which was the Essenes' ritualistic bathing for the forgiveness of sins ... which has clear parallels to the Christian rite of baptism."

"Wow, that is a strong similarity," said Punjeeh thoughtfully.

"And some scholars even argue that John the Baptist was once a member of the Essenes," Professor King added. "His monastic life in the Judean desert, his practice of baptism for the purification of the spirit, and his pronounced dislike of the Pharisees and Sadducees would have placed him in good company with the Essenes."

"Ahhh," said Punjeeh, "so the Essenes didn't like the Pharisees or Sadducees either."

Chloe nodded her head in confirmation. "Like the Christians later, the Essenes had strong disagreements with the Pharisees and Sadducees, but their dispute goes all the way back to the founder of the Essene sect, someone they called 'The Teacher of Righteousness.'"

"'The Teacher of Righteousness,'" Jack responded sarcastically. "That's a title that really makes a statement."

"Yes," Chloe replied, "and he was full of controversial statements, especially about the Pharisees and Sadducees, who he said were religious hypocrites, corrupt with power and beyond redemption, which is why he led his followers into the Judean Desert and formed the monastic community that produced the scrolls. But unfortunately for the Teacher, it appears some of these comments may have gotten him killed."

"Really," Jack quizzed, "what happened?"

"According to the Dead Sea Scrolls, the Pharisaic priests became jealous of the Teacher's following. They had him arrested, presumably on charges of heresy, and then put to death. In the eyes of the Essenes, the Teacher suffered a martyr's fate, and the scrolls suggest they never forgave the other two branches of Judaism for the death of their founder."

"And what ever became of these Essenes?" Punjeeh asked.

"We're not really sure," Chloe answered. "The Essene movement was founded by the Teacher around 150 BCE, and they survived at least until the time of Jesus. But after that, the trail grows cold. It's as if the Essenes just vanished. Scholars can only assume that they either died off or converted to Christianity."

Jack was impressed by Chloe's extensive knowledge about religion, but he was also anxious to go back to El-Amin. He was about to suggest they get going when he glanced down at the scroll one more time. It suddenly occurred to him that they had discussed every line of the scroll but one. "Hey guys, we didn't talk about this. What do you think it means?" He pointed to the line that read: *The Emperor's mother has descended upon Jerusalem and spread falsehoods.*

"Oh...yes," Chloe hesitated, attempting to sound surprised. Punjeeh read that part of the passage and shot a knowing glance to Chloe.

Jack witnessed their clumsy exchange, but he had no idea what it was about.

Oblivious to the situation, Professor King answered quickly, "Oh, right you are, Jack. That no doubt is a reference to Constantine's mother, Helena, or St. Helena as she became known, who went to Jerusalem right after the Council of Nicaea."

Jack harkened back to his visit the day before to the Church of the Holy Sepulchre. All of a sudden, he heard himself repeating, "St. Helena, the discoverer of the true cross."

Professor King was surprised at Jack's verbatim knowledge of a relatively unknown Catholic saint. "That's right, Jack," he said, "and that is her unofficial church title."

"There was a painting of her on display at the Church of the Holy Sepulchre," Jack explained. "I saw it yesterday."

"Oh, yes, of course," said Professor King with a chuckle. "I've seen that painting. She's depicted as a very beautiful young woman when she made her discovery. However, we do know that she was in her eighties when she traveled here, so the likeness in the picture is probably an exaggeration."

Jack suddenly felt a deep sense of concern. "So what falsehoods did she spread?" he asked hesitantly.

"Her assertion that she had discovered the location of Christ's crucifixion and tomb, of course," replied Professor King, looking somewhat surprised by the question.

Jack was dumbfounded. "You mean the church I went to yesterday isn't the site of Jesus' death and resurrection?"

"It's extremely doubtful, I'm afraid," the professor answered. "You see, there are all sorts of church legends as to how she was able to locate those sacred sites three hundred years after the fact: special visions, secret dreams, and the like. But unfortunately there's no credible historical or archeological evidence to back up her claims."

"Oh," said Jack, still trying to digest the news.

"And like I said earlier, Constantine was a shrewd politician," Professor King continued. "He wanted Christianity to be the religion of the empire, and that would require a strong presence in Jerusalem. He had a temple to the Roman goddess Venus torn down and the Church of the Holy Sepulchre built right on the same spot. In hindsight, we can see this as a foreshadowing of the future of religion in the Western world."

Silently, Jack remembered the strong emotions he felt when the guide explained the crucifixion process and when he saw the stone slab where Jesus' body was supposed to have lain.

Professor King sensed that Jack was troubled by the revelation and decided it was a good time to exit. He glanced at his watch. "I'm late for class," he said politely, "but do let me know how you make out at El-Amin."

They exchanged pleasantries with Professor King and assured

him they would let him know something as soon possible. After he left, Chloe turned to Jack and sighed. "I'm sorry, Jack."

Jack tried to play it cool. "What, are you kidding? It's no big deal. I didn't walk the route of Jesus; I just walked the route of Constantine's mom!"

Chloe giggled at his remark. She was glad he wasn't disappointed. "Would you mind if I come along with you to El-Amin?"

"Sounds great to me," Jack said as he looked over at Punjeeh for approval.

"By all means," Punjeeh confirmed.

"If you'll excuse me, I need to let the staff assistant know I'll be out the rest of the day."

Once Chloe had left the room, Jack acknowledged that he was more troubled by the latest revelation than he admitted.

"I'm sorry I didn't tell you what I knew about the Church of the Holy Sepulchre earlier, my friend," said Punjeeh. "But when you came back to the house yesterday I could tell you were very moved, and I didn't want to dampen the experience for you."

Jack made no attempt to hide his chagrin. "But what about all the people I saw there?" he asked bewilderedly. "Many were crying, so emotional and upset … and they had traveled from all over the world to see that place … Is it possible that all those people believe something that's not true?"

Punjeeh placed his hand on Jack's shoulder and looked deeply into his eyes. "It's like I said yesterday, my friend: Don't underestimate the power of belief."

# 16

Sue Merino, a forty-five-year-old middle-school teacher from Baltimore, was in her hotel room rummaging through the mountain of mementos and other souvenirs she had collected on her first trip to the Holy Land. Having dreamed for years about visiting the places where Jesus walked and talked, she was the first to sign up when Pastor Dan announced last fall that he would lead an expedition for all interested members of their congregation.

"Sue, how are you ever going to get all that stuff on the plane?" asked Mary, her roommate and leader of the church choir, as she gazed at the various items strewn across the bed.

"I don't know, but I just can't help myself. I want to buy everything!"

Mary sighed. "And did you get something from that kid on the beach yesterday, too?"

"Yes," she replied hesitantly, knowing Mary disapproved of her penchant for purchasing. She dug through her beach bag and pulled out the scroll. Unraveling it for the first time, she saw the cryptic writing on the faded paper. "It looks very old."

Mary was unimpressed. "How much did that cost you?"

"Five dollars."

"It looks like you got your money's worth." She glanced at the clock on the nightstand. "I'm headed down to the lobby. Don't be too much longer, we've got a big day ahead."

"Okay," Sue answered, "I'll be down in a minute."

‿ℳ‿

# 17

Tariq Mohammed had had a rough upbringing, even by Palestinian standards. Despite his intelligence and good looks, many of the families in Medina forbade their sons and daughters from associating with him.

This was because of his genealogy.

Tariq's father had been a senior member of the Jihadeen, a Palestinian terrorist group sworn to the destruction of Israel. When the Jihadeen claimed responsibility for a suicide bombing that killed fifteen people at a Jerusalem nightclub, the Israeli military bombed the family's home. Tariq and his father weren't there, but his mother and five-year-old brother were. They were both killed in the attack. Tariq was thirteen at the time.

A few days later, his father, distraught with grief, went on a merciless rampage in a Jewish settlement and was gunned down after a shootout with Israeli Special Forces. Tariq was left scared and all alone, and was fortunate that his aunt, Youseff's mother, agreed to take him in.

Being the son of a "martyred" Jihadeen guerrilla made for a difficult existence, especially for an orphan. To a fanatical few it was a sign of courage, but to most it was a scarlet letter.

It was late morning before Caleb and Youseff finally found Tariq walking out of the local corner store, noisily slurping a Coke and scarfing a chocolate bar.

"Where are they?" Caleb confronted him sternly.

Tariq wasn't intimidated. He peered down at Caleb and replied sarcastically, "Where's what?"

Caleb eyed Tariq's candy and soda and wondered where he had gotten the money for them. He hoped he didn't know the answer.

"Tell me you still have them," Caleb said as he stepped closer to Tariq, clenching his fists.

"Please," Youseff interrupted. "The scrolls, we know you took them from the tree. Now where are they?"

A smug smile pursed Tariq's lips. "Don't worry, I did you a favor and sold them in the tourists' market," he replied. "Here is your cut." He took a five-dollar bill from his pocket and held it toward the two boys, expecting them to be pleased.

Instead, his gesture sent Caleb into a tailspin.

"Five lousy dollars!" he yelled and grabbed Tariq by the collar, causing him to drop his candy and Coke.

Tariq reacted by grabbing Caleb's wrists and pulling them from his shirt. "What the hell is the matter with you?" he yelled. "Do you want to get hurt?"

Youseff quickly stepped in between, prying them apart. "Stop!" he screamed at the top of his lungs.

His uncharacteristic outburst caught them both off guard.

"Tariq," Youseff continued, "you shouldn't have done that. I trusted you and you betrayed me!"

"I did you a favor!" Tariq retorted quickly. "If you got caught with those scrolls, the Israelis would lock you up and throw away the key. Now take your money and be happy about it!"

"Tariq, you are so stupid!" Caleb said. "The old man was going to sell them for us for a lot more money."

"That old man is crazy," Tariq shouted." I told you two to stay away from him."

"He's an antiques dealer, Tariq," Youseff reasoned. "I think he knows more about these things than you do."

"That's not all he is," Tariq added with a look of disgust.

Caleb looked him straight in the eyes. "He has them sold for one thousand dollars each!"

Now it was Tariq's turn to be sick. "Oh my God," he said and faced Youseff. "Why the hell didn't you tell me that?"

"I didn't know then," Youseff said defensively. "Caleb talked to him again today."

"Wait a minute," Tariq said. "The old man has never even seen your scrolls. How could he say they are worth that much? This is all a bunch of lies."

"He didn't look at the scrolls but he looked at the jar," Youseff said.

Tariq gave him a confused look. "So?"

"Look," explained Caleb. "There was an archeological dig a long time ago that uncovered some jars like the one we found. They contained scrolls that were worth a lot of money. Come on, let's go talk with him. You can hear it for yourself."

The three boys hurried to the old man's curio shop. As they approached they could see Abu, a mentally impaired teenage boy, sweeping away the dust from the front porch. He meticulously stroked the broom from left to right across the concrete floor.

"Where is he?" Caleb asked as they got closer.

Abu didn't reply verbally. He stopped sweeping for a moment and looked up at the boys. His eyes were glazed and distant. He slowly raised his arm and pointed to the door.

"Thanks," Caleb replied hesitantly.

"That guy gives me the creeps," Youseff said under his breath as they went inside the shop.

"Me, too," Caleb agreed.

The old man was finishing a sale to a couple of Western tourists. The boys waited patiently as he punched keys on the cash register, took their money, and bade them farewell.

Once they left, the old man shifted his attention to his new visitors.

"Good morning, boys," he said with a smile while looking at Caleb and Youseff.

"Good morning, sir," Youseff replied.

The old man gave Tariq a less friendly look. "Hello, Tariq."

Tariq did not respond to his greeting.

"I was expecting you to come back yesterday," he said to Caleb. The long faces of the trio told him something was not right. "Good heavens, what's the matter? Did your parents find out about your cave expedition?"

"I wish that's all it was," Caleb said. "Tariq here took our scrolls and sold them to a couple of tourists today for ten dollars."

"I got fifteen dollars, actually," Tariq retorted.

"What?" replied the old man as the look of excitement fell from his face. "Tariq, how could you do that?" he scolded.

Tariq face reddened with anger. "I didn't know they were that valuable," he shot back.

"You must get them back," the old man replied while shaking his head disgustedly. "Where did you sell them?"

All three waited for Tariq's answer.

"I sold them down on the beach, at El-Amin."

"Who bought them?" the old man pressed. "Tell me everything."

Tariq gulped. "Two different people bought them. One was a woman, mid-forties maybe. She was tall, and a little fat. She said she was a teacher in the United States. I think she was staying at the hotel there on the beach, but she would be easy to pick out because she has an artificial leg."

"And what about the other person?" the old man hacked.

"He was an American man, he looked about thirty. He was just buying it to be nice, like he felt sorry for me or something," Tariq said. "I just played up to him and took the money."

"Yeah, all five dollars of it," Caleb said.

"Actually, I got ten from him," Tariq shot back.

"Stop it," the old man barked with authority. His stern tone silenced them both.

"Now, Tariq," he continued, "what else can you tell us about the American man?"

"He was with a friend who had the skin color of an Arab, but he was dressed like an American, and I think he said he was an emergency room doctor in Jerusalem. I saw them leave in a silver car, a BMW."

"That's just great," moaned Caleb in despair. "Even if we could find them we'll never get to Jerusalem. We can't get past the checkpoint."

"There are other ways into the city," the old man said assuringly. "But first, you three go and retrieve the scroll from the woman at the hotel. And you must do so today … right now."

"Well, how do we do that?" asked Caleb.

The old man looked at Tariq. "You persuaded her to buy it; perhaps you can persuade her to sell it back to you. And if that doesn't work, then why don't you enlist the help of a friend? That is, if the rumors I've heard around the village are true."

Youseff realized immediately what the old man was referring to. "That's a great idea," he exclaimed and looked over at Tariq for approval. "I had forgotten about her."

Tariq shot a stern glance back at the old man. "I don't know what you're talking about."

The old man spoke nostalgically. "Tariq, your father was a very great man. How will you turn out?"

Tariq erupted at the old man's remark. "You don't know anything about my father!"

"Calm down, Tariq," Youseff pleaded. "We wouldn't even be here if you hadn't taken the scrolls, so you've got to help us get them back."

The grim expression on his younger cousin's face pained Tariq. "I'll help you get them back," he replied. "But when I do, I'm gonna want a bigger cut."

"Whatever, Tariq," Caleb said desperately, "let's just get them back first!"

"Good, it's settled then," interjected the old man. "Now I want you three to go at once to the hotel, do whatever you need to in order to retrieve the scrolls, and return here immediately. Do not stay there after nightfall. In the meantime, I will see what kind of information I can find out about a dark-skinned emergency room doctor from Jerusalem."

# 18

Jack sat silently in the back seat as they left the college for El-Amin. The morning's events weighed heavily on his mind. While the potential value of the scroll and the sheer luck with which he had acquired it excited him, he was also stunned by the utterly unbelievable revelations it had unveiled in the process.

Were there really such deep divisions in the beginning of the Christian Church? What about the seemingly insane claim that the first Christians were Gnostics? And could it be possible that the Gnostics authored the most important parts of the Bible and were later overthrown by their Literalist counterparts? In a way, it reminded him of the countless examples in corporate America of company founders being ousted by overzealous board members who had "bigger and better" visions for the companies. But as crazy as it all sounded, something about the Gnostics' story was starting to seem plausible to him.

Punjeeh continued to discuss the day's findings with enthusiasm. "I can't believe this; it's really such an amazing find."

"I know. When Jack mentioned he had something for me to translate, I could never have imagined it would be something of this magnitude," Chloe answered.

"So what do you think the other scroll says?"

Chloe drew a breath. "I have a hunch," she said slowly, "but I don't know that I'm ready to voice it yet. I just hope we can get a look at it."

"Me too," Jack piped in from the back seat. "I should have just bought them both."

"I'm glad you're still with us, my friend," Punjeeh said while smiling at him in the rearview mirror. "I was starting to worry about you."

"I'm okay," said Jack. "This has just been a lot to take in."

Chloe was sympathetic. "I know, Jack. Examining religion from an academic standpoint rather than that of a practitioner can bring to light a very different picture from the one you learned in catechism. I admire your courage to do so."

Once again, Chloe's comments made Jack feel better, although he wasn't sure how courageous he was being. Throughout her explanations Jack became increasingly impressed with Chloe. Until today, Punjeeh had been the most knowledgeable person he knew on the topic of religion, but Chloe surpassed him hands down. He wanted to ask her about another topic that had been a source of confusion for him.

"I have a question about something else you mentioned this morning," Jack said, looking over at Chloe. "The ego, I'm not sure I understand what you're talking about there. What did the Gnostics mean by ego?"

Before she could answer, Punjeeh spoke up in a patronizing voice, "Jack, you've asked some dumb questions the past couple of days, but that by far takes the cake."

Jack was shocked, or better, he was enraged. Why would his old friend speak to him that way, especially in front of Chloe? Was he jealous of Chloe's obvious superiority of knowledge in this topic? Had Punjeeh not been driving, Jack was sure he would have punched him in the mouth. Instead, he retaliated verbally. "What the hell is your problem, you fat ass?"

Punjeeh bellowed with laughter. "Very good, Jack," he said, "and that, my friend, is a perfect example of the ego."

It quickly occurred to Jack what Punjeeh had done through his mock attack. His face turned red with embarrassment. "Oh, okay … you got me," he said sheepishly while looking at Punjeeh. "And I'm sorry I called you a fat ass."

"Why be sorry? It's true, I have gained some weight," Punjeeh replied good-naturedly. His expression then turned more serious. "Just see that the ego was the part of you that reacted to my statement; it was the part of you that felt injured. And for what? Some words out of my mouth? How could phonetic sounds from my vocal cords possibly cause harm to you?" Punjeeh turned to Chloe and grinned, "Sorry, professor, the opportunity was too good to pass up."

"That's one way to define the ego," Chloe agreed, "but I think the Gnostics' ideas about ego are broader than that."

"Really?" Punjeeh asked, once again intrigued by the Gnostics. "Please, tell us more."

Chloe paused while thinking of the best way to explain. "Do you remember what I said back in my office, about the Gnostics' claim that on an unseen level, there is a spiritual interconnectedness between all living things, that we are all part of the eternal One Life?"

Jack and Punjeeh nodded.

"The Gnostics said that the *ego* was the part of our consciousness that blocks us from seeing this Oneness. They taught that the ego is the source of our mistaken belief that we are separate entities, disconnected from and in opposition to the world around us. Furthermore, they taught that until one experiences gnosis, this disillusionment caused by the ego controls our life."

"That is deep," Jack said, raising his eyebrows, "really deep."

"I know," Chloe said with a smile. "And on a more basic level, they said that the two most common manifestations of ego are fear and desire, which they saw as the cause of virtually all human suffering."

"Professor King mentioned that this morning," Punjeeh remarked. "Could you elaborate a little more?"

"Specifically, the Gnostics taught that the fears associated with not getting something you desire or of losing something you already have are the underlying reasons why human beings cause harm to one another.

"Think about it, anytime in your life when you've hurt someone it's because you've felt threatened by them. Specifically, you were afraid that they were going to get something you wanted, or take something you already had, whether that was a material possession, social prestige, power, emotional security, or what-have-you."

Jack thought about his own life for a moment and realized what Chloe said was true.

"The Gnostics taught that when you truly *know God*, or experience gnosis, the ego dissolves. And when it does, all fear and desire dissolve with it. They say that only then does one realize the connectedness of all things, and it becomes impossible for you to hurt another human being, because you see that every time you hurt someone else, you are in fact just hurting yourself. The Gnostics claimed that this was the deeper meaning of Jesus' famous statement '*Do unto others as you would have them do unto you.*'"

Jack and Punjeeh pondered this.

Finally, Punjeeh spoke up. "So it's all about experiencing gnosis, eh?"

Chloe remained silent.

"And how does one experience this gnosis?" Jack asked.

"That part is the mystery," she replied with a twinkle in her eye.

Jack looked out the window toward the Old City and saw a sign pointing the way to the Church of the Holy Sepulchre. His experience there yesterday now felt like a dream.

"The other things you and Professor King said this morning were surreal...I mean, not that the whole thing with Helena 'discovering' the tomb isn't bad enough, but Constantine combining stuff from other religions and changing another god's birthday to Christmas. I had no idea."

"That all may sound unsettling to us now," she answered, "but it was a fairly common practice in those days for religions to borrow traditions and images from one another. Constantine wasn't the only one to incorporate other religions' symbols into Christianity. The Gnostics appear to have done that, too."

Jack frowned, "Like what do you mean?"

"The Christian use of the dove as a divine symbol may also have had its origins in Greek and Roman religions."

"But that doesn't make sense," Punjeeh interrupted. "The origin of the dove in Christianity is obvious. The biblical gospels relate how the Holy Spirit came down from heaven in the form of a dove and hovered over Jesus as he was being baptized by John. And in the Old Testament, Noah released a dove from the ark in order to find dry land."

"You're absolutely right," said Chloe, "the Bible does tell those stories. But for centuries prior, the dove had also been a symbol of divinely inspired peace and love from the goddesses Venus and Aphrodite. There is no doubt that people in the ancient world were familiar with this older association. And if we accept the Gnostics' claim that they authored the gospels, then perhaps the dove was a calculated inclusion in the Jesus baptismal story."

Chloe's last comment immediately bothered Jack. "Wait a minute, a *calculated inclusion*? Are you implying that the dove may not really have hovered over Jesus like it says in the Bible, but that the Gnostics wrote it in for effect?"

"Given the association of the dove as a sign of divinity in the ancient world, I think it is certainly a possibility to consider," she answered. "Don't forget, Jack, the Gnostics were very different from the Literalists. They claimed that the historical accuracy of the gospels was not as important as understanding Jesus' inner message. Given that assertion, do you think a Gnostic author would have had a problem with adding the image of a dove, a well-known sign for divine peace and love, to make a point about Jesus and his teachings?"

Jack contemplated her question for a moment. "I don't know, maybe not. I had just always believed that everything in the Bible was completely true."

Chloe understood his predicament. "Of course you have, and that's because you grew up in the Literalist tradition. You've been spoon-fed the idea of the historical infallibility of the Bible since you were a young child. Try to take a step back from that belief for a moment.

"If you suddenly found out that the Holy Spirit did not assume the form of a dove and descend out of the heavens as recounted in the Bible, would that change anything about the beauty of Jesus' message?"

Jack thought aloud, "I guess not. It's just difficult to let go of the belief that it actually happened."

"I couldn't agree more, my friend," Punjeeh added. "Beliefs can become so ingrained in us that we oftentimes can't see the forest for the trees. And look where that can lead – in this country opposing belief systems are at the root of all the violence."

Punjeeh's last statement reminded Jack of their discussion the day before. He wondered what Chloe thought. "So has Punjeeh told you his opinions on beliefs?"

"He's shared a little with me," she replied. "And his comments are timely for our discussion of the Gnostics, especially in regard to their views about beliefs and the ego."

"How so?" Punjeeh asked.

"The Gnostics held that beliefs and the ego were closely related," she continued. "They said that the ego was the only part of the human psyche that felt the need to claim one set of beliefs as exclusively right and another as necessarily wrong. And like you, Punjeeh, they saw this type of behavior as destructive."

"Well, there, Jack," Punjeeh beamed. "I'm in good company after all."

Chloe grinned. "Yes, the Gnostics' adherents were encouraged to question their personal beliefs as they progressed along the spiritual path, because they taught that it was often one's internal beliefs that were the final block to experiencing gnosis."

The loud ring of Punjeeh's cell phone interrupted their discussion. "Hello, this is Dr. Kohli."

Punjeeh listened to the caller. Within seconds, his expression changed, and Jack knew something was seriously wrong.

"That's horrible," Punjeeh said sadly into the phone. He listened intently to the caller and then added, "Please let me know if you need another set of hands, and I'll come right away...Okay, thank you. Goodbye."

Jack and Chloe waited for an explanation as Punjeeh hung up.

"That was a colleague of mine. There's been another suicide bombing, about an hour ago at a bus stop in downtown Jerusalem. Half a dozen people were killed and several more injured."

"Do you need to go?" Jack asked.

"No, he said there was nothing I could do."

"That's such a tragedy," Chloe added.

Jack could tell by the tone in her voice that Chloe was very disturbed by the news. Remembering how he felt after the attacks on the Pentagon and the World Trade Center, he imagined how difficult it must be to live in an area where this type of violence occurs on a regular basis.

"I know it must be tough living here with all the bombings," said Jack in an attempt to be comforting.

"Yes, it can be very worrisome at times, but I haven't lost hope that this will all come to a peaceful conclusion someday."

Punjeeh was not as optimistic. "It's like I always say...just another day in the Holy Land."

# 19

The only hotel at El-Amin beach was a long, three-story tan stucco building with a barrel tile roof. Jack hadn't paid much attention to it on their first trip here, but he was anxious to get inside now. Punjeeh explained on the ride out that the hotel was owned by a French company and was mainly a weekend getaway for Israelis. Most Americans preferred the major hotel chains in Jerusalem, and he was surprised that a tour group from the United States had found this one.

As they drove down the semicircular drive and under the hotel's front awning, Punjeeh lowered his window for the young Palestinian bellhop that came out to greet them.

"Welcome to the Château by the Sea," he said, "Are you checking in?"

"No," replied Punjeeh, "we're just here to see a guest."

"May I park your car?"

"Please."

As the three began to exit the vehicle, Jack had an idea. "Say, maybe you can help us," he said to the bellhop. "We're looking for an American woman, a tourist, fortyish, brown hair, a little on the heavy side. She's traveling with a tour group."

The bellhop shrugged his shoulders. "I'm sorry, sir, I see so many people. Perhaps you should check at the front desk."

"This woman's a little different," Jack continued. "She has an artificial leg, from about here down." He placed his hand just below his knee.

The bellhop's expression was blank. "I'm sorry, sir, I'm afraid I didn't notice anyone like that."

"Okay, thanks anyway," Jack replied.

As they walked through the entryway, Jack surveyed the hotel's layout. The front desk was straight ahead, a restaurant was off to the right, and big glass doors to the left opened out to the courtyard and beach. "Let's look around down here first. Why don't you and Chloe check the beach?" Jack said, pointing outside. "I'll look in the restaurant. We can meet back here in a minute."

They split up and Jack quickly scanned the hotel's eatery. There was no sign of the schoolteacher from Baltimore. He walked back to the lobby but Punjeeh and Chloe had not yet returned from the beach. A small dark-skinned man working at the front desk had noticed the trio initially and now offered his assistance. "Can I help you, sir?"

As Jack was about to answer, Punjeeh and Chloe entered through the beach doors. Punjeeh shrugged his shoulders, and threw up his hands.

"I hope so," said Jack as he walked up to the front desk. "We're looking for an American woman. I believe she is staying here at your hotel."

"Of course," said the man cordially as he turned to his computer keyboard. "And what is the name?"

"Well, that's just it ... I don't exactly have her name."

The man raised his eyebrows at Jack's answer. His tone changed immediately, from gracious to snooty. "Well, I'm sorry then, sir, but I'm afraid I can't help you."

Jack was never one to take no for an answer. "But this is kind of an emergency," he persisted. "Perhaps if I describe her you'll remember ... "

"No, sir," the clerk responded quickly, cutting him off. "For security reasons we're not allowed to give out any information about our guests."

Upset that he wasn't getting anywhere, Jack decided it was time to resort to more persuasive measures. He reached for his money clip, peeled off a one-hundred-dollar bill, and placed it on the counter.

"Like I said, this is kind of an emergency." He slid the bill across the counter in the direction of the clerk.

The clerk looked down at the bill, then glanced from side to side to see if he was being watched. Satisfied that he wasn't, he grabbed the bill from Jack and stuffed it quickly in his jacket pocket. "Well, I'm really not supposed to give out information about our guests, but we have only one American tour group staying with us right now, and they are out for the day."

"Where did they go?" Jack responded quickly.

"Bethlehem," he replied. "They left about an hour ago but their tour guide said they would stop at some of the shopping districts along the way. Even so, I would imagine they'll be arriving at the Church of the Nativity anytime now, and I don't expect them back at the hotel until this evening."

Jack remembered reading about the Church of the Nativity in his guidebook, as its construction marked the spot of Jesus' birth. He looked back at Punjeeh and Chloe. "Can we go there?"

"Of course, it's only a twenty-minute ride from here," Punjeeh replied, nodding to Jack and the clerk.

Jack turned back to the clerk. "Thank you, you've been very helpful."

"Of course, sir," replied the clerk, nodding ceremoniously.

They headed quickly out the front of the hotel toward the bell stand. Once they were out of earshot, Chloe shrieked, "Jack! You're incorrigible!"

Jack laughed, "I really don't like the word no."

"I'm sorry, Chloe," Punjeeh added sarcastically. "I should have warned you ... Jack is full of surprises."

The bellhop saw them approaching. "Did you find who you were looking for, sir?"

"Looks like she's out for the day," Punjeeh replied. "So we're off to Bethlehem to catch up with her."

"Very good, sir. I'll get your auto right away."

As the bellhop retrieved their car, Jack commented, "Hey, in a way this is great. I mean Bethlehem was second on my list of places to go. I can't wait to see Jesus' birthplace and the Church of the Nativity."

Punjeeh and Chloe's expressions instantly changed. "What?" he asked hesitantly, glancing between the two of them.

Chloe bit her lower lip. "Well," she said, "it's just that Helena *discovered* that, too."

Jack stopped dead in his tracks. "That's just freakin' great! So tell me, is there anything to see here that Constantine's mom didn't *discover*?"

Punjeeh let out a bellowing laugh and slapped Jack on the back. "Poor Jack, you just can't catch a break."

***

As the bellhop returned with the car, a public bus slowed in front of the hotel for its early-afternoon El-Amin stop. From a window toward the rear, Tariq watched as the silver BMW he saw the day before pulled out of the hotel entrance with Jack, Punjeeh, and Chloe inside.

"Look!" he said to Youseff and Caleb. "That's the American and his friend who bought one of the scrolls."

Caleb and Youseff rushed to look out the window as the car sped away.

"I wonder what they were doing in the hotel," Caleb added.

They rushed from the bus and headed to the hotel entrance. One benefit of living in a small Palestinian village is that everyone knows everyone. When they got close enough, Caleb yelled out to the bellhop, "Rasoul, those people who just left, are they staying here?"

"No," the bellhop answered. "They were here looking for some American tourist woman with a fake leg, but she went to Bethlehem for the day so they were going there to find her."

"They know," Tariq said when he heard Rasoul's answer. "They know what they have now, and that's why they are looking for the American woman."

Caleb agreed. "I bet you're right."

"So what are we going to do?" Youseff asked.

Tariq stopped to think. "Hopefully she didn't take the scroll with her. Maybe I can find out what room she's in and we can get it back before it's too late."

The other two boys looked at each other uncomfortably. "You mean steal it back?" Youseff asked.

Tariq gave them a stern look. "Do you have a better idea?"

# 20

The Palestinian city of Bethlehem was not as Jack had imagined. Home to fewer than twenty-five thousand residents, it lacked the curb appeal of the well-maintained Old City of Jerusalem. The vacant downtown streets were lined with boarded-up businesses and buildings badly in need of paint jobs.

Punjeeh explained that the poor conditions of the city were partly due to the steep decline in tourism revenue, which had dropped off significantly since the Palestinian-Israeli conflict had intensified in recent years. Now Bethlehem was known more for its frequent skirmishes between PLO fighters and Israeli soldiers than its extravagant Christmas celebrations.

Unfortunately, the Church of the Nativity was not immune to the conflict. A recent incident involved a group of Palestinian gunmen who took refuge in the church to escape pursuing Israeli forces. The Jewish army surrounded the church, and the ensuing standoff lasted several weeks. Eventually a settlement was negotiated without bloodshed, but it did nothing to end the bitter feelings between the two sides. While Jerusalem was certainly ground zero in the conflict, Bethlehem wasn't far behind.

As they arrived in the vicinity of the church, the dismal downtown setting brightened somewhat. Many more vendors were operating in the shops and on street corners around the church, catering to Christian pilgrims willing to brave the unpredictable environment.

"There's the church," Chloe said as she pointed to the stone building at the end of the street. Jack noticed a big difference between the Bethlehem church and the shrine he visited the day before, as the Church of the Nativity was nowhere near the behemoth structure of the Holy Sepulchre. The unremarkable white rock edifice was only two or three stories high, dwarfed by most of the churches he had attended back home.

Punjeeh drove into the visitors' parking lot. As they climbed out of the car, and headed for the church entrance, Jack peered up at the modest structure with the small bell tower. "So, Chloe, what's the story with Helena and this place?"

"Very similar to what happened in Jerusalem, really," she answered as they continued walking. "After Helena finished her expedition there, Constantine ordered the construction of the Church of the Holy Sepulchre. She then traveled here to Bethlehem to *find* Jesus' birthplace ... " Pointing to the church in front of them, she added, " ... and this is the spot she came up with."

"So what makes people think this isn't the place?" Jack pressed.

Chloe raised her eyebrows skeptically. "A better question might be what made Helena think it was. Remember, she arrived here more than three hundred years after Jesus' birth, and just like in Jerusalem, there's never been any historical or archeological evidence to support her findings."

Punjeeh's brow wrinkled as he remembered something else from their earlier conversation. "And the Church of the Nativity, did Constantine have it built, too?"

"Yes, he did," Chloe answered, "and that's another reason why scholars doubt the authenticity of Helena's finding."

Jack didn't see the correlation. "What does that have to do with anything?"

"If you remember, Professor King explained this morning that in Jerusalem Constantine had a temple to the goddess Venus torn down so the Holy Sepulchre could be built in its place. A similar thing occurred here with the Church of the Nativity."

"It was constructed on a site that was sacred to another god of ancient Greece, Adonis. In fact, when Helena arrived here in the fourth century, the popular legend was that Adonis was born here."

Punjeeh and Jack exchanged surprised glances. "He was born here in Bethlehem?" Jack asked.

"That was the legend," Chloe answered. "Adonis was said to have been born out of the trunk of a myrrh tree." She quickly scanned the courtyard in front of the church. "Like the one over there." She pointed to a squatty tree with yellowish-green leaves.

"And what happened to the ancient temples here and in Jerusalem was not uncommon," she continued, "because after Constantine's conversion to Christianity, Greek and Roman temples across the empire were demolished so Christian churches could be erected in their place, but nowhere more notably than here, Jerusalem, and Rome, where the legendary home of the Roman gods, the Pantheon, was converted into a shrine for the Virgin Mary. Constantine even ordered the construction of St. Peter's Basilica on the site of a Roman religious cemetery, and the adjacent temple to the god Mithras was destroyed to make room for the Vatican."

"*The* Vatican?" Punjeeh asked incredulously. "Are you saying that was previously the site of another god's temple, too?"

"Yes. And as you probably know, the centerpiece of the Vatican is believed to have been constructed on the grave of Jesus' disciple, St. Peter. But just like with the birth and crucifixion sites of Jesus, historians and archaeologists have no reason to think Constantine located Peter's actual burial site. These scholars find it odd that within a very short period Constantine's agents *discovered* some of the most important sites in all of Christianity, all more than three hundred years after the events were said to have taken place. Not to mention the most remarkable coincidence that all these sites were located where existing Greek and Roman religious temples stood, all of which had to be torn down, of course."

"Naturally," smiled Punjeeh.

"So the lack of any real archaeological evidence to support Constantine's finds has led many scholars to argue that the location and construction of these Christian churches are more a testimony of Constantine's determination to replace the other religions of the empire with Christianity, rather than a genuine concern for locating and commemorating true historical sites."

As Chloe finished her last statement they reached the entrance of the church. Jack returned his focus to the task in front of them. "That's mighty interesting; now let's get inside and look for the woman with the other scroll."

They hurried through an unusually small front door into the church's foyer. Jack briefly stopped and stared into the church's central chamber, a rectangular hall about the size of a small high-school gymnasium. Two sections of wooden pews sat under towering twenty-foot ceilings, and about two dozen giant stone columns lined the side walls. The pews faced a humble altar aglow with candles. The only windows were small and near the ceiling, allowing for very little light.

The trio moved quickly back and forth across the stone floors, pretending to examine the paintings and statues along the side walls while really scanning the faces and appendages of the handful of women who were present. Unfortunately there was no sign of the schoolteacher.

"Maybe they're still shopping." Jack remembered that the hotel manager had said they planned on shopping along the way. He had noticed numerous roadside boutiques on the drive over from the hotel.

"It's quite possible," Punjeeh concurred. "Esther can spend hours in those shops."

"We haven't looked for her downstairs yet." Chloe pointed to a room to the right of the altar. "That's where Helena said the birth took place."

Jack and Punjeeh followed her into the adjoining room, a small domed hall with an opening in the floor. Inside the opening was a steep flight of stairs that looked like they led directly under the altar. To the right of the stairway was a large statue of a stately looking man in priest's attire.

"Ah, St. Eusebius of Caesarea," Chloe said and gestured to the statue, "and how appropriate for our discussion today."

"Who?" Jack asked, not even attempting to repeat the pronunciation.

"U-Sib-E-us of See-zuh-REE-uh," Punjeeh said distinctly, sounding it out for Jack's benefit. "He is considered the father of church history."

Chloe raised her eyebrows. While impressed with Punjeeh's recitation, she disagreed with his conclusion. "Eusebius is often referred to as the father of church history, but I think a more fitting title for him would be the Minister of Propaganda."

Punjeeh laughed heartily. "Okay, Chloe … you'll need to explain that one."

"Bishop Eusebius was Emperor Constantine's right-hand man," she explained, "and was perhaps the single most influential priest of all time. At the Council of Nicaea, he was a major advocate for the consolidation of the church and the Roman Empire. Afterwards, he became Constantine's official biographer, where he coined the term 'Constantine the Great.'

"And you're right, Punjeeh, he also wrote the only surviving history of the early Christian Church, called the *Ecclesiastical History*, which became accepted as fact by virtually all Christians for the next fifteen hundred years."

"And I'm guessing by the title you've bestowed on him that it wasn't an objective history?" Punjeeh asked humorously.

"That is putting it mildly," she replied. "But in Eusebius's defense, he states at the onset of his account that his intention is not to be fair or balanced, but instead to discredit those who claim to have *so-called Special Knowledge of God.*"

Jack's eyes widened. "The Gnostics?"

"Exactly," Chloe replied. "Eusebius was vehemently anti-Gnostic and was determined to eliminate their claim that they were the original Christians. Not surprisingly, his history of the early church succinctly portrayed the Gnostics as heretics and depicted Literalism as the original form of Christianity. And once the Gnostics were killed and their writings destroyed, subsequent generations of Christians had no reason to doubt that his account of the early church was factual."

Punjeeh shook his head. "Until hearing what you said this morning, I had no reason to doubt him either."

"He was also a central figure in the development of what the Catholic Church calls the Doctrine of Apostolic Succession, where Eusebius claimed to accurately trace the lineage of ordination of all the Literalist church bishops back to Jesus' twelve disciples."

"Of course," Punjeeh said. "Apostolic succession is kind of like a family tree for the clergy. It's a record of who ordained whom, and is supposed to go all the way back to St. Peter and Jesus."

"Very good, Punjeeh," Chloe confirmed, "and the Literalist church used the Doctrine of Apostolic Succession as a political tool, claiming that since their priests could trace their ordination lineage back to Jesus and his disciples, this proved they were the original Christians. But modern scholarship has shown that the pedigree offered by Eusebius is much less fact than fiction."

Chloe gazed at the unremarkable face chiseled out of stone. "I know he doesn't look like much, but Eusebius was a key player in Literalism's ascent to power. He understood that for the Christian movement to be great it needed a clearly defined written history, and that's what he gave the Literalist church. Constantine, for his part, provided the military might and built landmark churches in Jerusalem and Rome. Unfortunately, modern scholarship has shown that both of these men had little regard for the truth, but were more concerned with advancing their own political agenda."

"I wonder if they ever believed it themselves," Jack commented.

"What would be the difference?" Punjeeh asked.

"It's hard to find many good things to say about Eusebius and Constantine," Chloe added. "In addition to being anti-Gnostic, Eusebius was severely anti-Semitic. His writings blamed the whole of the Jewish people for the crucifixion of Jesus and were cited as justification for the murder of Jews through the next several centuries. And while some historians still refer to Constantine as 'The Great,' a title bestowed on him by Eusebius, no one can dispute that it was under his rule that Christianity first became a religion of war. He had a cross emblazoned on every soldier's shield in the Roman army and killed thousands of people in the name of Jesus... and for reasons that are unknown to historians, he even had his own wife and son executed!"

Jack was disgusted. "My God, that's terrible."

The three stood in the uncomfortable silence that often occurs when people contemplate the incomprehensible acts committed by their fellow human beings. Punjeeh was the first to speak, motioning to the opening in the floor. "Shall we take a look down below?"

The stairs fed into a dimly lit small room. The air smelled damp and musty. The walls were lined with various shrines and ornate paintings of Catholic saints. Directly across the room stood a larger shrine marking the location of Jesus' birth. The few tourists who were present in the lower level had gathered there, but unfortunately none of them resembled the middle-school teacher from Baltimore.

"She's not here," Punjeeh concluded.

"There is an adjoining room we can still check," Chloe said, pointing to the entrance of a small passageway on the opposite wall.

As they walked into the center of the room Jack's eyes adjusted to the darkness. He could now see that the walls and ceilings were bare earth and rock. It was then that he realized where they were. "But this is a cave," he said with bewilderment and stopped in his tracks.

"Were you expecting a manger?" Chloe asked with a hint of sarcasm.

"Well, yes, I guess so."

"Don't feel bad, my friend," Punjeeh chuckled. "That's what I thought the first time Esther and I came here. But the tour guide explained to us that in those days animals were often cared for in caves. They were used much like a modern-day barn or stable."

Punjeeh looked over at Chloe for confirmation, but he could tell by the look on her face that it wasn't coming. "That's one theory," she said skeptically, "but I think there is a far more credible explanation."

Punjeeh and Jack exchanged glances.

"It was common belief among early Christians that Jesus was born in a cave," she said as she raised her hand and pointed to the earthen ceiling above. "But as time went on, the cave setting of the nativity story became a problem for the Literalist church. They were troubled by all the, umm...*prior associations*, so to speak...so ultimately, the cave was dropped and the scene was described as a manger instead."

"What prior associations are you talking about?" Punjeeh asked.

"Just like what I said about the dove being a well-known symbol in the Greek and Roman religions, several of the Greek and Roman gods were said to have been born in caves, too. The ancients considered caves a symbol for the birth canal of Mother Earth. The births of the gods Mithras, Dionysus, and Zeus were also said to have occurred in caves."

Punjeeh's eyes brightened as he followed Chloe's suggestion to its logical conclusion. "So do you think placing the scene of Jesus' birth in a cave was a *calculated inclusion* by the Gnostics?"

Chloe smiled, impressed by Punjeeh's ability to connect the dots. "Yes, I think that's very likely. The idea that Jesus was born in a cave would have signaled to people in the ancient world that he was a divine being, and that fit the Gnostic pattern of borrowing other religions' iconography."

Jack was resistant. "How can you be so sure? If caves were used as stables, like the guide said, then maybe Jesus really was born in a cave."

"It's possible," she acknowledged. "But I think the argument that it was a calculated inclusion gets stronger when you examine the other aspects of Jesus' birth story, most of which are virtually identical to older religious traditions."

Jack felt an uncomfortable twinge run down his spine. "Like what?" he asked.

"First and foremost, the virgin birth. This was a popular motif in the ancient world, as several of the Greek and Roman gods were also said to be born of virgins. Based on the ancients' cultural obsession with female sexual purity, the theme of an immaculate conception was quite commonplace when it came to divine births."

"You've got to be kidding me," Jack blurted out.

"Not at all," Chloe replied with an innocent look on her face. "Dionysus, Attis, Horus, Apollo, and Perseus were all said to be the result of a virgin birth. In fact, one story that bears striking resemblances to the Jesus birth can be found on a wall in the ancient Egyptian temple in Luxor, where hieroglyphic inscriptions written hundreds of years before the New Testament gospels recount the birth of the Pharaoh Amenophis, who was also considered the son of God. The story goes that when Amenophis's mother was a young woman, she was visited by a divine spirit who told her she had been chosen for a special mission, and although a virgin, she would soon give birth to a divine child."

"That sounds just like the biblical Annunciation," Punjeeh exclaimed, "when the Angel Gabriel appeared to Mary and told her she would give birth to Jesus."

"That's right," said Chloe. "And that's not all. The hieroglyphics go on to say that shortly after Amenophis's birth, he was visited by three kings bearing gifts."

Punjeeh was stunned. "Just like the three wise men who brought gifts to the infant Jesus," he said nostalgically, as if he had repeated the story again and again but was finally hearing it for the first time.

Jack felt dazed by the revelations. He followed slowly as they navigated the narrow passageway and entered the adjoining cavern. Much to their chagrin, it was empty of tourists, filled only with more shrines, statues, and altars.

"You were right, Punjeeh," Chloe concluded. "They must not have arrived yet." She scanned the iconography around the room. "But while we're here, there are a couple of things I'd like to show you."

Chloe looked past Jack's shoulder to an altar against the wall. "Over here," she said as she walked toward the altar. "Take a look at this statue."

Jack hesitantly followed her to the altar and immediately recognized a white marble sculpture of a seated Virgin Mary, holding the infant Jesus on her lap. It was virtually identical to the ones he had seen throughout Catholic churches all his life.

"Statues that look almost exactly like this were found in the catacombs of ancient Rome and date back to the early Christian era. But they *weren't* Mary and the baby Jesus. They were the Egyptian goddess Isis and her divine son Horus. It seems that the early Christians saw such a striking resemblance in the Egyptian portrayal of the holy mother and her divine child that they worshiped them as Mary and baby Jesus, without changing a thing!"

"It could all just be a coincidence," Jack countered, feeling a need to say so for his own benefit, if not anyone else's.

"There were many other similarities," Chloe continued. "The birth of Mithras was said to be witnessed by three shepherds and announced by the appearance of a miraculous star. Unusual celestial occurrences had been a well-known symbol to herald divine births throughout the Greco-Roman world for centuries."

"Just like the star that proclaimed the arrival of Jesus in the Gospel of Matthew!" Punjeeh exclaimed.

"Exactly," Chloe confirmed.

She pointed across the room to another white stone altar and motioned for them to follow her.

"Do you remember the biblical story of the evil King Herod, who allegedly ordered the murder of all male babies in Bethlehem after learning that Jesus had been born?" she asked, glancing between Jack and Punjeeh.

"The Slaughter of the Innocents," Punjeeh answered again. "It's one of the most horrifying stories in the New Testament."

"That's right," Chloe responded. "And the room we're standing in is called the Chapel of the Innocents, dedicated centuries later to the alleged victims of that event. But I have some good news.

Scholars are quite certain that this travesty never occurred, as this type of story was prevalent throughout antiquity when recounting the great perils in which certain gods and kings were born on earth. There have been several legendary accounts of evil rulers ordering the mass execution of male babies upon hearing that a divine savior or king has been born."

"This is utterly fascinating," said Punjeeh. "I can't believe I've never heard these similarities before."

"Yes," Chloe concluded. "Legends of virgin births, miraculous stars, visits from wise men and shepherds, the mass execution of male heirs and the like, all appeared in older religious traditions that were well known throughout the Roman Empire at the beginnings of Christianity, and certainly the gospel writers knew these stories too."

Jack was speechless by this time.

Punjeeh, on the other hand, was full of questions. "So your suggestion is that none of these things actually happened to Jesus, but that the Gnostics included them when they wrote the gospels because that would have appealed to the people they were writing for?"

Chloe nodded her head. "I think it's the most logical explanation...because if you look closely you'll see that virtually nothing in the account of Jesus' birth was original, but instead was taken from older Greek and Roman religious traditions...and this type of borrowed symbolism was in keeping with the Gnostics' pattern."

Jack couldn't keep quiet any longer. "I shouldn't even be listening to this," he retorted as wave after wave of negative emotions rushed through him. "It's ridiculous."

Now Chloe was stunned. "I'm sorry, Jack," she said, seeing for the first time how upset he was. "I didn't mean to offend you. I thought you wanted to know these things."

Jack sat down on a bench beside the altar. He, too, was mystified at his reaction. Having always prided himself on being open-minded, he quickly acknowledged his mistake. "No, I'm the one who's sorry," he said, shaking his head quickly. "I don't know where that came from." He looked around the room at all the altars, shrines, and statues of various Catholic saints. "I think I just feel kind of funny talking about this here, like it's sacrilegious or something,"

Punjeeh knelt in front of the bench and looked Jack in the eye. "Tell me, Jack, do you feel guilty?"

Jack stared back at his old friend. He knew instantly that Punjeeh had hit the nail on the head. "Yeah, I guess in a way, I kind of do," he replied.

"Well there's no guilt in the truth, Jack," Punjeeh assured him. "Yesterday you believed in some things that you are finding out today may not be true..." He paused for a moment, "Where's the guilt in that?"

Jack thought about what his friend said. He knew it made sense. Punjeeh held out his hand. Jack took it and Punjeeh pulled him to his feet. "You're right," Jack said.

Punjeeh smiled.

Jack, still embarrassed by his outburst, turned to Chloe. "I'm sorry, Chloe, that was really unlike me."

"It's okay," she said compassionately. "These things can be upsetting when you hear them for the first time."

"There's a small bistro directly across the street from the church with outdoor seating," Punjeeh interjected. "Why don't we get a table there and we can watch for this woman's arrival."

"Good idea," Chloe concurred. "And we can always head back to the hotel and wait for her there; the hotel employee did say her group would be returning this evening."

Jack agreed that was a good plan. He looked back through the passageway they had traveled toward the main cavern. "Well I came all the way here from the U.S.—I'm at least going to see the *alleged* site of Jesus' birth," he quipped, trying to lighten the mood he had created.

Punjeeh grinned. "That's my Jack," he said, slapping him on the back.

They backtracked to the main cave, where tourists were gathered around the large shrine at the base of the north wall. As Jack approached, he saw a white patch of marble in the floor with a shiny silver star inlaid in the middle. Decorative oil lamps were suspended on silver chains from the ceiling and hovered in a semicircle above the star.

Jack was struck by the artistic uniqueness. "It's beautiful," he said.

"I couldn't agree more," Chloe replied.

She leaned over and whispered into his ear so as not to disturb the other visitors. "And so is the symbol it stands for...I hope you understand that I don't think the importance of Jesus' message is contingent upon whether or not the story of his birth happened just like it says in the Bible. To me, it doesn't change anything about what Jesus represents."

Jack turned his head and looked at her. He could see the deep sincerity in her eyes. "Thank you," he replied.

# 21

Back at the hotel, the younger boys waited on the beachside walk-way while Tariq went around back, slipped in the employee entrance, and made a beeline for the housekeeping department. As he did, a beautiful young Jewish girl was just beginning her afternoon shift, pushing her cleaning cart down the hall toward the service elevator. Upon seeing Tariq, a scowl hardened her face. "What are you doing here?"

Tariq pretended to be surprised at her hostility. "Dalya...I came to see you, of course."

Dalya was unmoved. Dating Tariq was difficult enough because of their differing religious backgrounds. She was from a working-class Jewish family, and although they were not Orthodox, her parents frowned upon her dating a Muslim. And while she found Tariq charming, sometimes irresistibly so, his unaccountability was proving too much to handle.

"I'm fine," she replied coolly. "I've been working, which is probably more than I can say for you. And where have you been? I haven't heard from you in more than a week."

"You have a right to be upset," he replied remorsefully. "I'm sorry I haven't contacted you...I've meant to, I promise. I shouldn't have come to see you here at work. I'm sorry."

He lowered his head, spun around slowly, and had taken about three or four steps when she called out, "Wait."

Dalya was unable to see the sly smile that parted his lips. He turned around and walked back to her. "Thank you. That makes me very happy." He reached down and grabbed her hand, pulled it to his mouth and kissed the back of it. She blushed when he did so, once again experiencing the warm feelings she had missed.

Tariq continued to hold her hand and make small talk for the next few minutes, asking about her family, job, and complimenting her big brown eyes. As he did, Dalya slowly let her guard down. Finally, he inched toward the real reason for his visit. "And believe it or not, I did come to see you yesterday, but I couldn't find you."

"You did?"

"Yes … but it's probably all for the better, because it was a terrible day anyway."

"Why? What happened?"

"Well, my cousin found two old scrolls in the desert, and I sold them to some American tourists on the beach here yesterday for a few dollars … only to find out later from the antique store at the village that they are worth one thousand dollars each."

"Two thousand dollars!" she marveled as her eyes lit up.

"Yes, and I'm sure they have no idea what they bought. You know how the Americans are … "

Dalya shrugged. "Maybe you can buy them back from them, if you can find those Americans again."

Tariq looked at her with feigned surprise. "You know … that's an excellent idea! And I believe one of them is staying here at the hotel."

Dalya had always been gullible when it came to Tariq's charm, but she would have to have been sedated not to see through him this time. She quickly pulled her hand back. "That's why you came here, isn't it? It's not to see me! It's just to get your stupid things back!"

Tariq felt a genuine sadness envelop him. He had never desired to cause Dalya any pain. The truth was that he really did like her, and that's the reason he was so sporadic in contacting her. When you lose everyone who is close to you, a defense mechanism often develops whose sole function is to destroy any chance of future intimacy, and in turn limiting your own ability to be hurt. But for some reason, he now heard himself being honest with her. "Okay, the truth is that I have missed you … I really have … but right now, I do need your help."

"Forget it, Tariq. I could lose my job, and that's important to some people," she scolded him.

"I'm really sorry, Dalya … and please, I took the scrolls from Youseff so I need to do this for him, too."

"That's not my problem, Tariq."

"Look, I know that there aren't a lot of Americans who stay at this hotel...she's a middle-aged woman, light-skinned..."

"That describes almost all of them," Dalya replied.

"But this lady has an artificial leg ... Do you know the woman I'm talking about?"

"Maybe," Dalya said, knowing immediately whom he was referring to.

"The American man who bought the other one was downstairs in the lobby looking for her. He must have figured out that the scrolls have value...I'm such an idiot," Tariq said.

Dalya could feel herself wanting to help him.

"Rasoul said the American was going to Bethlehem to find her. My guess is he wants to get the other scroll from her. If I don't get it back now, it's gone forever...Can you please just look in her room and tell me if you see it? Then just tell me the room number and I'll take over from there."

Dalya drew a deep breath. "Wait here," she said, against her better judgment. "I'll see what I can do."

# 22

Feelings of guilt lingered in Jack as the trio made their way from the Church of the Nativity to the small bistro across the street. Guilt's presence in religion had always perplexed him. It was like the omnipresent specter floating in the background, and for reasons he never really understood. But Punjeeh's words of comfort continued to ring in his head: *"If it's true, why feel guilty?"*

The temperature was in the upper nineties by now, but fortunately all the patio tables had sun umbrellas. The absence of humidity in the Palestinian desert air made even the hottest days bearable, as long as one was in the shade. They chose the table closest to the front, which offered an unobstructed view of the church parking lot and entrance.

"We can see everything from here," Punjeeh noted.

"Yes," Jack agreed. "I hope she shows up soon."

"Don't worry, my friend," Punjeeh assured him. "We'll find her."

Once seated, the waiter came over to take their drink order. After requesting three ice waters, Punjeeh turned the conversation back to Chloe's latest revelations. "The things you told us in the church were utterly amazing. I can't believe I've never heard of those similarities before."

"That's the understatement of the year," Jack said woefully.

Chloe smiled. "They say we only hear things when we're ready to."

Punjeeh could tell that Jack was still bothered by the revelations in the cave. "Is there anything you'd like to talk about, my friend?" he asked, placing his hand on Jack's shoulder.

"It's just a lot to take in," Jack mustered. "I was so overwhelmed with fear and guilt back there ... Where do you think all those feelings came from?"

Punjeeh shifted the question back to him, "Where do *you* think they came from?"

Jack was silent for a moment. "I'm not sure... but I guess I thought that by listening to Chloe's explanations I was betraying God, or that maybe He'd be angry with me for even entertaining the idea that some of the things in the Bible aren't true."

Jack could tell by Punjeeh's expression that this was the answer he wanted to hear. "That's an honest response, my friend... but let me ask you, what is the foundation that makes those feelings of guilt and fear possible?"

Jack had to think again. Then it occurred to him what Punjeeh was pointing to, although he wasn't sure he agreed. "My beliefs?"

"Could it be anything else?" Punjeeh replied.

Jack produced a half smile. "I should have known you would come back to this."

"Let's examine it for a moment, Jack," Punjeeh answered in a more serious tone. "You feel guilty *only* because you adopted a set of beliefs that you now think you have betrayed. In other words, what would happen if you didn't have those beliefs? Would you still feel guilty?"

"I guess not," Jack said hesitantly.

Punjeeh tried to think of another way to explain his point. "Look here," he said as he pointed down at the menu in front of him. "If you order a ham sandwich for lunch today, would you feel guilty about that? Would that constitute a betrayal of God's teachings for you?"

"Of course not," Jack replied quickly.

"I didn't think so," Punjeeh replied. "Yet you do realize there are thousands of people within a ten-mile radius of us who believe exactly that, and maybe even someone right here at this table." Punjeeh looked at Chloe.

Jack quickly remembered that Islam and Judaism forbid the consumption of pork. "But this is altogether different from that," Jack retorted. "How can you compare believing in the Immaculate Conception to eating a ham sandwich?"

Punjeeh laughed good-naturedly. "My friend, you may think I am comparing a felony to a misdemeanor, but I'm sure there are several devout Muslims and Jews who would disagree with you."

Jack realized his last comment might have been out of line. He looked over at Chloe, hoping she wasn't offended. "I'm sorry, Chloe, I didn't mean that like it sounded."

"It's fine, Jack. No offense taken."

Jack turned back to Punjeeh. "But don't our beliefs define who we are?"

Punjeeh leaned in as his expression turned serious again. "Do they, Jack?" he asked rhetorically. "Or is it more accurate to say that you, I, and almost everyone else on this planet blindly accepted a set of beliefs from the environment in which we grew up? It's as if they were deposited in us as small children... and there comes a time when one has to examine those beliefs to see which, if any, are really true for *you*."

Punjeeh's last admonition struck Jack, as he had never considered the possibility that some of the things he had been brought up to believe in might not be true for him.

Their conversation was interrupted by the waiter's return. "Are you ready to order?" he asked Punjeeh as he set down the glasses of water.

"I think so," Punjeeh replied. "I'll try your hummus."

The waiter turned to Jack, who had been too engrossed in the conversation to look at the menu. "Oh... I'll try the same," he added.

"And for you, miss?" he asked Chloe.

"I'll have a ham sandwich," she said, flashing a sly grin to her surprised companions.

Punjeeh chuckled aloud as the waiter departed. "I must say, Chloe, you are full of surprises... and after our conversation in the cave, I'm wondering what other revelatory information about the Gnostics and early Christianity you are keeping from us."

Chloe's smile changed as she looked over at Jack with hesitation. He immediately picked up on her reservations. "No more outbursts, I promise," he said as he raised one hand and placed the other on a menu, as if taking a solemn oath.

His humorous gesture put her at ease. "Okay, Jack, but remember, you asked for it."

Jack felt another twinge run down his spine. He hoped he could keep his promise.

"Before we go any further," she added, "I think it is important to discuss the religious climate in which Christianity came into being."

"That would be very enlightening," Punjeeh agreed.

"I know it seems strange to us now," she began, "but when the religion of Christianity first emerged, almost everyone in the Roman Empire believed in many gods, not just one. In addition, god worship differed based on the geographic region in which one lived. There were different gods worshiped in Egypt than in Rome, and still different ones in Greece than in Asia Minor."

"I remember reading about some of those gods in college," Jack said. "It's hard to believe people took all of that seriously."

"It does seem strange to us now, having grown up in a monotheistic tradition," Chloe agreed, "but I can assure you, with the exception of the philosophers and intellectuals of the ancient world, most everyday people were convinced these gods were real. And with so many gods, it's not surprising that a 'competition' of sorts emerged between them, or perhaps I should say between their followers."

"Competition?" Jack quizzed.

"Yes, a notion that 'my god is more powerful than yours,'" she answered, then paused again. "And one way the ancients measured the superiority of one god over another was by their ability to perform miracles."

Punjeeh realized immediately where she was headed. "So if gods had to perform miracles to demonstrate their power, what does that say about the amazing feats Jesus did in the gospels? Like changing water into wine, healing the sick, or raising people from the dead."

"That's an excellent question, Punjeeh," Chloe replied, "and any examination of the gospels and potential *calculated inclusions* by their Gnostic authors would be remiss without discussing the miracles they attribute to Jesus, as there were many older stories of other gods and their agents commanding the same type of power. In fact, the ones you just mentioned are an excellent place to start."

Jack and Punjeeh waited in silent anticipation.

"The Gospel of John reports that Jesus' first miracle was the changing of water into wine at a wedding celebration in nearby Cana. However this miraculous feat was already well known in the Greek-speaking world, because for centuries the same story had been ascribed to the Greek god Dionysus, who was also said to have regularly changed water into wine. In fact, this miracle was so commonly attributed to Dionysus that he even became known as the God of Wine.

"And given the sad state of medicine in the ancient world, Doctor, the ability to miraculously heal the sick was another popular measure of a god or holy man's power. For instance, the Roman Emperor Vespian, who like many other Roman emperors was believed to be divine, is said to have cured blindness by making mud with his spittle and rubbing it on the eyes of the afflicted, the same way Jesus is said to have cured a blind man in the Gospel of Mark.

"Along those same lines, the ancients had very little knowledge of mental illness, instead believing the afflicted had become 'demon-possessed.' In one well-known Greek religious ceremony, followers of the goddess Demeter were said to have had two thousand evil demons cast out of them and sent into a herd of pigs, just as Jesus cast two thousand demons into a herd of pigs in the Gospel of Luke."

Punjeeh marveled in her revelations. "This can't be mere coincidence," he reasoned.

"But by far the most important miracle a god could perform in the ancient world was to raise the dead ...," Chloe said and stopped briefly. "And not surprisingly, there are many, many stories of gods and holy men and women performing just this type of miracle.

"For instance, the Greek holy man Empedocles is said to have revived a woman after she had been dead for several days, just as Jesus is said to have raised Lazarus from the dead several days after his passing. And Apollonius of Tyana, another first-century holy man whose followers claimed he too was the son of God, is said to have healed the sick, raised the dead, and most notably, resurrected the young daughter of a Roman official without visiting her, much the same way the gospels recount how Jesus revived the slave of a Roman army officer without ever seeing the body."

Jack was again unnerved by the information. "So you don't think Jesus really did any of these miracles, is that your point?"

"I'm saying that there were so many stories in the ancient world of gods healing the sick, casting out demons, and raising the dead that the Christian movement would hardly have been taken seriously if Jesus could not do the same. Consequently, it seems more likely that the gospel authors added these miracle stories and others like them to their account of the life of Jesus in order to attract more followers to the newly formed Christian religion ... and this fits well within the Gnostic pattern."

Jack again felt an internal need to defend his rooted beliefs, but he was conscious to be more objective this time. "But you can't say for sure that Jesus didn't perform these miracles, right?"

Chloe understood. "That's true, Jack … I don't know how anyone alive today could say for sure whether Jesus actually performed the miracles recounted in the gospels. All we can say with certainty is that miracle stories such as these were common in the religions of antiquity. And in an age where people relied on magic and miracles to explain the uncontrollable events taking place around them, it's easy to understand how gods and religious figures were often relied upon to heal the sick, cast out demons, and raise the dead."

Jack remained still, deep in thought. He could see the logic in Chloe's words, but there was something he didn't understand. "But if what you say is true, weren't the people who told these stories just lying to everyone?"

Chloe paused. "I think your criticism is well placed," she replied. "And if my hypothesis is correct, then it's clear that the gospel authors weren't being literally truthful. However, if we accept the Gnostics' claim that they were the first Christians and authors of the gospels, we must also remember that they never intended the gospels to be used in the way the Literalist church later would.

"The Gnostics taught that one only believed the virgin birth and miracle stories in the beginning, when first becoming a Christian. Later on, the Gnostic initiate would realize that many of the stories recounted in the gospels were not historical events, but had simply been a necessary first step to place them on their journey.

"But when the Literalists seized power," Chloe continued, "they insisted that belief in these types of events was the end of the spiritual path, not the beginning."

Jack had been keeping his eyes on the church throughout their conversation. He now noticed a large tour bus pulling into the church parking lot and stopping near the back, about a hundred yards from where they were seated.

He tapped Punjeeh on the shoulder and pointed. "Look!"

Punjeeh and Chloe turned and saw passengers beginning to exit.

Jack stood and squinted, scrutinizing the movements of each person who exited the bus. Suddenly he noticed a female figure with a distinct limp being helped off the bus by a fellow passenger.

"There she is!" Jack exclaimed.

Punjeeh held his hand up to his forehead to block the sun as he focused his eyes in the bus's direction. "Are you sure?"

"That's her, it's a definite! Get the bill!" Jack commanded and bolted from the table.

He ran out the café's patio entrance and into the street, causing cars in both directions to slam on their brakes and honk their horns.

"Jack! Be careful!" Chloe shrieked.

Jack waved his hand in apology to the perturbed drivers as he continued in a gallop across the street and into the church parking lot.

The passengers had their backs to him as they headed for the church's entrance. He could see the woman with the limp, and although she wore long pants, he knew it was she.

Once Jack was within a few yards he called out, "Excuse me, ma'am!"

The woman and her female companion stopped and turned around.

"Yes?" she asked, puzzled.

Jack's spirits deflated immediately. "Oh…I'm sorry. I thought you were someone else."

"No problem," answered the genteel-looking woman in her early thirties. Now that they were close he could see that her foot was in a boot-type cast.

Jack turned around and looked back to his friends, who were standing at the table watching his every move. He raised his hands above his head and waved them down, signaling the false alarm.

Jack trotted back across the church parking lot, consciously looked both ways before crossing the street, and joined his friends on the café's patio.

"That was quite a show you put on, my friend," Punjeeh chuckled.

"Yes, Jack, I would like to see that scroll as much as anyone," admonished Chloe, "but it's not worth someone getting killed over."

"Sorry," Jack offered. "I guess I got a little caught up in the moment."

"Patience, my friend," Punjeeh chided him.

They resumed their seats as the waiter arrived with the order. After taking a few bites of the hummus, which he and Punjeeh agreed was not as good as Esther's, Jack turned the conversation back to Chloe's latest revelations. "What you've said today is still so hard for me to believe, because I have always been taught that everything in the Bible is completely true... that it was the infallible word of God."

Chloe smiled slightly and washed down a bite of her sandwich with a drink of water. "Please don't take this wrong, Jack, but it's generally those who know the least about the Bible that always refer to it as *God's infallible word*."

Jack was surprised by Chloe's frankness, although he knew that at least in his own case, she was right.

Punjeeh chuckled. "I think she has you on that one, my friend."

Chloe looked at Punjeeh. "I wouldn't get too full of yourself just yet, Doctor. For someone who professes so much interest in the subject, I've been very surprised today at your own information deficiency."

Punjeeh stopped laughing. "Oh... well, I..." He started to defend himself and then decided against it. "Touché, my dear Chloe... touché."

Jack was happy to see Punjeeh take a little abuse for a change, and he decided to bring some humor into their discussion. Ceremoniously clasping his hands in front of his chest in a prayer position, he bowed his head and said, "Please, Professor, enlighten us about the Bible!"

Punjeeh laughed at Jack's gesture. Chloe looked at Punjeeh and asked, "Does he always act this way with people he's just met?"

"Only the ones he likes," replied Punjeeh.

"Okay then, Jack," she responded good-naturedly, "shall we continue to discuss just the gospels, or perhaps the Bible as a whole?"

"Uhhh ... " said Jack hesitantly, "and what's the difference again?"

Punjeeh roared, "I think he just made your point, Professor."

Chloe rolled her eyes and swallowed another bite of food. "Let's take it from the top, shall we?"

"The word *bible* is Greek. It means *books*... and that's exactly what the Bible is, a collection of books by different authors... and these books are divided into two parts, the Old Testament and the New Testament.

"The Old Testament is a collection of sacred Jewish scripture, all of which concern the teachings, history, and development of the Jewish religion. The stories of Adam and Eve, Noah's Ark, and Moses parting the Red Sea are all recounted in the Old Testament."

"Right, right," Jack said, as her explanation triggered a memory from his high school days, "and the New Testament ... it's all about Jesus, right?"

"That's correct," Chloe replied. "It begins with four books that are called the gospels – namely Matthew, Mark, Luke, and John – and they are universally considered to be the most important Christian books, since they are the only ones that provide a narrative of the life of Jesus and his teachings."

"And you think that it was the Gnostics who wrote these gospels?" Punjeeh asked.

"I do," Chloe replied. "The inclusions of fictitious events like the virgin-birth narrative and miracle stories suggest that in spite of what the Literalist church later claimed, the authors of the gospels were not concerned with limiting their work to a fact-based historical account of the life of Jesus. Instead, it appears more likely that their goal was to attract new followers to the fledgling Christian religion by appealing to religious motifs popular at the time. This pattern is very much in line with Gnostic ideals."

"You're starting to convince me," Jack conceded, dipping into the hummus.

"And there are further clues in the gospels themselves to support this view," she hinted, and could tell immediately by Jack and Punjeeh's expressions that they were eager to hear more.

"For instance, despite the fact that the Gospel of Mark appears second in the New Testament, almost all scholars agree it was actually the first written, somewhere around 70 AD."

"So about forty years or so after the time of Jesus," Punjeeh commented.

"That's right," she confirmed. "And it wasn't until ten to twenty years after Mark that the Gospels of Matthew and Luke were written, followed finally by the Gospel of John.

"And while there are pronounced similarities in all four of the biblical gospels, the first three written in chronological order – that is Mark, then Matthew, and then Luke – present what scholars now call *The Synoptic Problem*."

"What's that?" Jack asked.

"It refers to the fact that these three gospels are so similar in story line and wording that it's impossible for the latter two to have been written without extracting substantial material from the former."

Punjeeh looked lost. "Wait a minute. Are you saying that Matthew and Luke copied text from the Gospel of Mark?"

Chloe nodded her head in confirmation. "Yes, undoubtedly. Even the most conservative scholars agree that the authors of the Gospels of Matthew and Luke plagiarized extensively from the Gospel of Mark, as there is paragraph after paragraph of identical wording."

Jack was stupefied. "But why would they do that?" he asked.

"That's a good question. And you see, while the Gospel of Mark is the oldest of all the biblical gospels, it is also the most basic. Quite simply, the literary skill of the author of Mark was not up to par with the authors of Matthew and Luke—the latter two authors were much better writers. So in an apparent effort to improve the image and message of Christianity, they reworked the text from Mark, greatly improving the style and grammar, and as we discussed earlier, added a few items."

"Added a few items?" Jack asked.

"Yes, because it's only the Gospels of Matthew and Luke that recount the miraculous events associated with Jesus' birth. The Gospels of Mark and John begin with Jesus as an adult. This has allowed scholars to pinpoint the place where the virgin-birth story entered into the popular account of Jesus' life, and it wasn't until the second and third gospels."

"I didn't realize that," Jack replied.

"It sounds like the Gospels of Matthew and Luke were basically the *new and improved* versions of Mark." Punjeeh said sarcastically.

"I guess you could put it that way," she replied, finishing her sandwich.

Jack was trying to process all this new information when he remembered something else from his catechism days. "But I thought the gospels were written by some of Jesus' disciples?"

"No," Chloe replied quickly, "scholars are sure that none of the gospels were written by eye witnesses, as it was a common practice in ancient times to write something anonymously and assign its authorship to a figure who was supposed to have been present at the actual events. For instance, the gospels state that Jesus did have a disciple named Matthew, but it is very unlikely he is the same person who wrote the biblical Gospel of Matthew, as the Literalist church later claimed."

"Why do you say that?" Punjeeh questioned.

"For one reason, it is precisely a passage describing an interaction between Jesus and Matthew that the author of Matthew copies from Mark! If the author of Matthew were one of Jesus' disciples, why would he copy someone else's account of his own activities?"

"Good point," Punjeeh agreed.

Jack also conceded it was tough to dispute that logic.

"And there is something else that was very troubling about the Gospel of Mark for the Literalist church," Chloe added, "so troubling that they decided to change the ending of this gospel more than three hundred years after it was written!"

Punjeeh and Jack exchanged startled glances.

Excited, Chloe continued. "If you read the Gospel of Mark carefully, you'll notice that the twelve disciples never realize that Jesus is the Messiah until the very end, or not until the last ten verses. But the problem is that the original Gospel of Mark did not contain these final verses! They were added by the Literalists centuries later!"

"But why on earth would the Literalists add a new ending?" Punjeeh's voice rose.

"That's simple," she replied. "To refute the Gnostics' claim that they were the original Christians."

Jack and Punjeeh's bewildered looks let her know they needed more explanation.

"The Literalists needed the new ending to substantiate the Doctrine of Apostolic Succession we discussed earlier. Remember, the Literalist church claimed that their clergy were the only true carriers of Jesus' teachings because all their priests and bishops could trace their ordination lineage back to the twelve disciples themselves. So can you imagine what a quandary this created for the Literalist church when the Gospel of Mark ends before the disciples ever realize that Jesus is the Messiah?"

Punjeeh was astonished. "Of course! If the Literalist church based its claim of being the original form of Christianity on the Doctrine of Apostolic Succession, and the first and oldest of all gospels ended without the apostles ever realizing Jesus was the Messiah, what does that say about their claim to power?"

"Exactly. The Literalist church had a special motivation in making sure the apostles were redeemed in the Gospel of Mark, the oldest of all biblical gospels, since they claimed their version of Christianity descended directly from these twelve men. Consequently, they added ten new lines at the end to ensure this was done."

Jack shook his head in disbelief. "Plagiarisms, added endings, borrowed stories from other religions...and this whole time I had never really questioned what was in the Bible."

Chloe sympathized with Jack's plight. "It's important to remember that the books of the Bible were written by human beings, and that the Literalist church fathers didn't compile them into the current volume until more than three hundred years after the time of Jesus."

"And when you say the Literalist fathers compiled the Bible, do you know who in the Literalist church did so specifically?" Punjeeh asked.

Chloe shot him a baffled glance. "You mean you really don't know?"

Punjeeh was embarrassed. "Ah, no...," he said. "Should I?"

"I think I do." Jack looked like he'd solved a mystery.

Chloe's surprise grew into shock. "Yes, Jack?"

"It was that Eusebius fellow, wasn't it?"

Chloe exhaled. "Well, Jack, I am impressed."

Jack looked at Punjeeh. "She said he was the most influential priest of all time. Who else could it be?"

Punjeeh slapped Jack on the shoulder. "You're catching on, my friend, you're catching on."

"And although he didn't sign his name as the editor," Chloe continued, "there is little doubt about Eusebius's influence in the selection of writings that were included in the New Testament, as it was shortly after his death that the current Bible first appeared, or the mid-fourth century."

"My dear Chloe, you've given new meaning to the phrase *gospel truth*," Punjeeh added sarcastically.

Just as Punjeeh finished speaking, Jack caught sight of a group of people exiting the café. One of the group headed straight for their table. Before Jack realized what was happening, a vaguely familiar voice blurted, "Well, hello again!"

# 23

"Fancy meeting you here," Sue Merino said and smiled from ear to ear. "Have you been to the church yet?"

"Uh, no...I mean, yes," Jack stammered, his mind suddenly blank as he realized the woman they had been looking for had been inside the café the entire time.

"We got here a while ago but decided to get something to eat before going into the church, but I can't wait to get inside," Sue continued.

Three other members of her tour group, one male and two females, walked up as she was talking. She turned to them and said, "I met this young man on the beach yesterday outside our hotel. He's from Virginia, and his friend here is a doctor." She motioned to Punjeeh. The other group members smiled at the trio.

Jack quickly regained his composure and rose from the chair. Punjeeh and Chloe followed suit. "I don't think I properly introduced myself yesterday. My name is Jack Stanton," he said. "This is my friend Dr. Kohli, and this is Chloe Eisenberg, a religion professor at the University of Jerusalem."

"Hello," Chloe greeted them politely.

"I am Sue Merino, and these are my friends Mary and Judy, and this is Pastor Dan, the leader of our expedition. As I mentioned, we're from Baltimore." Mary and Judy were also middle-aged and conservatively dressed. Pastor Dan was a heavy-set man, mid-sixties, about six feet tall with graying beard and hair.

"Baltimore is a beautiful city," Jack said, attempting to make small talk before revealing that their meeting again today was not a chance encounter. "Which church do you attend?"

"The Church of the Holy Spirit," Pastor Dan answered enthusiastically, his speech revealing a slight Southern drawl. "We're just a simple Bible-believing church."

"Oh," Jack said, "that's great."

"It must be fascinating to be a religion professor here in the Holy Land," Judy said admiringly to Chloe.

"I enjoy it very much, thank you," she replied modestly.

Jack glanced over at Chloe and Punjeeh, whose faces made it clear that they were waiting for him to make the first move. Jack turned back to the schoolteacher from Baltimore. "I must confess, Sue, we didn't come here today just to visit the church. The hotel manager said I might be able to find you here."

"Oh? Whatever for?" Sue's eyes widened.

"It's regarding the scrolls we purchased from the boy on the beach yesterday. I asked Professor Eisenberg here to have a look at mine, and she thinks it may be have been written by the Gnostics."

Sue's blank expression indicated she had never heard of the Gnostics, so Jack attempted to explain. "They were an early group of Christians that— "

"We know all about the Gnostics," Pastor Dan broke in.

"Oh, great!" Jack exclaimed.

"Heretics," he hissed, "every last one of 'em."

Jack was dumbfounded by Pastor Dan's remark. An acute awkwardness fell over their gathering. Jack did his best to rebound. He looked back at Sue. "Oh...well, as I was saying, yours may have been written by the same group. Would you consider letting us take a look at it?"

"What for?" Pastor Dan challenged them. He glanced over at Chloe and Punjeeh. "Nothing against you folks, but there is enough misinformation out there already from the so-called educated class about the Gnostics. I don't mind telling you, they were nothing but liars and troublemakers...wolves in sheep's clothing!"

Jack had had enough. He was about to tear into Pastor Dan when Chloe broke in. "I couldn't agree more, Reverend," she added in her best professorial tone, "and I'm sure these scrolls will provide further evidence that the Gnostics' ideology was, in fact, a heresy."

It was hard to tell who was the most stunned, Jack and Punjeeh, or Pastor Dan.

"Well, I do say, Professor," Pastor Dan replied, "it's a refreshing change to hear a voice of reason coming from the academic community." He smiled and nodded deeply toward Chloe.

"You're quite welcome, Reverend," Chloe said. "I hope you can understand now why we would like to have a look at this scroll."

Everyone turned and looked at Sue, who had been eerily silent since Jack first mentioned the scroll. She now spoke in a strained, hesitant voice. "Well, I would be happy to give it to you, but the truth is, I threw it away this morning."

"You did what?" Jack blurted out.

"Mary and I were talking, and I've already bought so much stuff, there was no way I could get it all in my suitcase."

"Did you throw it away at the hotel?" Punjeeh asked calmly. "Perhaps we can still retrieve it."

"Yes, I did, in my room this morning. We're in room 153. And the nicest young girl has been cleaning our room. She's probably emptied the trash by now but perhaps she can track it down for you."

Jack thought quickly. "At least let me buy it back from you." He reached into his pocket and fished out his money clip, then pulled a twenty-dollar bill off the top and extended it to Sue. "For your trouble."

"Oh no," she replied, "that's way too much. I paid only five dollars for it."

"Then you just made a three-hundred-percent return," Jack replied with a grin. "Consider it a donation to your church." He looked over at Pastor Dan and smiled.

"In that case," Sue lowered her eyes and accepted the money. "I hope you are able to find it."

"I think we'll head back there right away and see if we can track it down," Jack said.

As the group said their goodbyes, Jack flagged down the waiter and paid the bill. Once Pastor Dan and his group were out of earshot, Punjeeh whispered, "Jack, my friend, I never thought I'd say this, but I think I've met someone who is a bigger bluffer than you are!"

Jack laughed. "Yes, I think I've met my match."

They both looked at Chloe. "It's like I always say," she replied, "people only hear what they are able to, so it's pointless to tell them anything else."

"Very true," Punjeeh agreed.

Jack was still reeling from Pastor Dan's remarks. "What was that guy's problem, anyway?"

"He represents an extreme point of view," Chloe offered. "I think most Christians today, if they knew about the Gnostics, would agree with much of their philosophy."

"He's got to protect his belief system," added Punjeeh, "no more, no less."

Jack thought of the scroll. "And can you believe she threw it away?"

"Don't worry," Punjeeh assured him, "worse-case scenario it's in the Dumpster at the hotel."

As Punjeeh finished speaking, the waiter returned with Jack's change. "Thank you for coming in," he said. "And please be careful–they just announced on the radio that there has been another suicide bombing."

"Besides the one this morning?" Punjeeh asked incredulously.

"Yes," the waiter replied. "Just a few moments ago in a Jewish neighborhood in Tel Aviv. They say that four or five people were killed and a dozen or more were wounded."

"Gosh," Jack exclaimed as the waiter departed. "This place is like a war zone."

"No ... this place *is* a war zone," Punjeeh corrected him.

"Do you need to get back to the hospital?" Chloe asked.

"I don't think so," Punjeeh answered. "Tel Aviv is more adequately staffed than Jerusalem, but I will phone in to make sure." Punjeeh walked to a more secluded part of the patio to make the call.

"I didn't realize the impact this conflict has on people's everyday lives here," Jack commented.

"Yes ... it makes you look around and think every time you're in a public place."

Punjeeh returned. "They do not need me now, but asked that I stay close by in case something else happens. The attacks appear to be co-ordinated and they are afraid there might be more. Let's hurry back to the hotel and see if we can't get our hands on that other scroll."

# 24

Punjeeh gunned the engine as they left the Church of the Nativity. He lowered his visor to block the setting sun. "You need to come and see me more often," he said to Jack, eyeing him in the rear view mirror, "I haven't had this kind of excitement in a long time."

"Glad I could oblige," Jack replied.

"And as for you, Chloe," Punjeeh continued, "I grew up well-versed in Catholic doctrine, believing that the Literalist church was the creation of the original followers of Jesus, and that Gnosticism was a later heretical offshoot. But you have made a convincing case today that the opposite is true."

Jack leaned forward from the back seat. He was still unsure how all the pieces fit together. "I can understand what you're saying about the Gnostics being the original Christians, but I'm confused as to how the Literalists developed after them."

"I'll see if I can summarize for you," Chloe answered. "Modern scholarship suggests that the first Christians were an esoteric group of people who believed Jesus was the son of God, or the long-awaited Jewish Messiah. Furthermore, it appears that some of these early followers borrowed stories from older Greek and Roman religious traditions, like the virgin-birth and miracle stories, and attributed them to Jesus in an effort to attract people to Christianity.

"As more and more people converted to the new religion, these original followers planned to share the deeper meanings of Jesus' teachings, what they called the 'secret mysteries,' with the new converts as they became ready to hear them."

"Like the Secret Mystery mentioned in the first scroll?" Punjeeh asked.

"Exactly," Chloe responded. "But sadly, it appears that many of the new Christian converts weren't interested in the deeper under-standings of Christianity that were encapsulated in the secret myster-ies, instead opting for a literal interpretation of the gospel stories."

"And these are the people who then became known as the Literal-ists?" Jack interrupted.

"That's correct. And as is the case with most religious movements, a class of professional priests quickly emerged among the Literalist be-lievers. These priests began to teach their followers that the gospels were historically infallible documents, despite the fact that many of the stories contained in them were preexistent in other religious traditions."

"Something that is really quite amazing when you think about it," Punjeeh chimed in.

Chloe's expression turned solemn. "But unfortunately, it wasn't long before those who claimed to know the secret mysteries of Je-sus' teachings, now called Gnostics, became greatly outnumbered by their Literalist counterparts.

"To make matters worse, some in the Literalist church, like the Heresy Hunters, became very jealous of these Gnostics and their claims of being the original Christians and having secret knowledge of Jesus' teachings."

"Jealousy…Why else would they have wanted to silence them so badly?" Punjeeh asked rhetorically.

"And the coup d'état for the Literalist church was in 326 AD," she continued, "when the Emperor Constantine converted to their form of Christianity, insuring that the Literalist priests would enjoy the power and backing of the Roman government."

"Sounds like game over to me," Jack commented.

"With the full support of the Roman government, the Literalist church branded the Gnostics as heretics, condemned them to death, and went about destroying all their writings, which effectively erased any trace of their claim as Jesus' original followers. The Literalist Bishop Eusebius, Constantine's personal biographer and right-hand man, then rewrote the history of the early Christian Church, naming the Literalists as the original Christians and the Gnostics as a later he-retical movement…and unfortunately, it's this history that has sur-vived in the minds of almost all Christians until the present day.

"But the discovery of the Gnostic writings at Nag Hamadhi some fifty years ago turned our view of the early Christian Church upside down, casting serious doubt on Eusebius's version of early church history and making the theory that the Gnostics were the original Christians very plausible.

"And one more thing to remember – the classifications of Gnostic and Literalist didn't come about until the second century, once the split became apparent. The original followers of Jesus, whom I have been referring to as the Gnostics, did not refer to themselves as such."

This puzzled Jack. "So what did they call themselves?"

Chloe turned her head to look him squarely in the eye. "Simple. They called themselves Christians."

"Oh," Jack replied with surprise, "I guess that makes sense."

Punjeeh adjusted the AC, and the cool air began to blow forcefully through the front and rear vents. "Chloe, I'd like to play the devil's advocate for a moment. You've made a very convincing case that some of the first Christians were Gnostics and that they borrowed heavily from Greek and Roman religious sources, but until a moment ago you've said almost nothing about Christianity's Jewish roots. Tell me, why would the Jewish followers of Jesus borrow so much from non-Jewish sources?"

"I was wondering when somebody was going to ask that question." Chloe winked at Jack. "And while you're absolutely right, Punjeeh – Christianity is undeniably of Jewish origin – it sounds like you are unaware of a crucial piece of Jewish history."

"Really? And what might that be?" Punjeeh asked.

"The Jewish Diaspora, or the great dispersion. The phrase refers to the huge exodus of Jews from the Holy Land beginning in the sixth century BC, when Jerusalem was first conquered by the Babylonians. These displaced Jews eventually spread out and formed communities all around the Mediterranean, in what would later become the Roman Empire. By the time Christianity emerged on the scene five hundred years later, there were actually more Jews living outside of present-day Israel than living within it.

"And in large part, due to the territorial conquests of the Greek ruler Alexander the Great, the ancients who lived throughout the Mediterranean world became heavily influenced by Greek culture.

This included the Jews living throughout the diaspora, many of whom had never been to Jerusalem, and who, after generations of living away, had become infused with the ideas and religious beliefs of those they lived amongst–the Greeks."

"So you think that's where they came up with the stories about the virgin birth and the miracles then, right?" Jack asked.

"Exactly," Chloe replied. "The generations of Jews that lived amongst the Greeks would have heard countless stories of virgin births and miraculous feats by the gods of Greece and Rome."

Chloe looked out the side window at the rocky hills of the Judean Desert and the jagged, sand-colored cliffs that had remained unchanged since before the time of Jesus.

"Not far from here is the village of Qumran," she said enthusiastically, "the home of the Jewish Essenes who produced the Dead Sea Scrolls. And although the Essene movement was begun here by the Teacher of Righteousness in 150 BCE, his followers would later form communities in Rome, Corinth, Thessalonica, and Galatia, and these communities would have been fertile mixing ground for the beliefs of Judaism and Greek and Roman religious traditions."

Something in Chloe's last sentence rang a bell with Punjeeh. "Wait a minute," he said. "Those cities are also the locations of the first Christian churches, to which St. Paul addressed his biblical letters."

Chloe smiled again. "That's right. St. Paul, universally accepted as the person most responsible for spreading Christianity throughout the ancient world, addressed his biblical letters to the Romans, Corinthians, Thessalonians, and Galatians, but I believe that these Christian churches were converted Essene communities."

"What makes you think so?" Punjeeh queried.

"Besides the practice of baptism and their belief that the Messiah would be a holy man rather than a warrior-king, there were many unique linguistic parallels between the Essenes and the first Christian communities. For example, unlike any other sect of Judaism, the Essenes referred to their communities as the *Church of God*."

Punjeeh picked up on the reference immediately. "The Church of God was the same title St. Paul used when writing about the first Christian churches!" Punjeeh exclaimed.

"That's right," Chloe verified, "and what's more, the Essenes were the only Jewish sect to call all their members saints, another Pauline reference to all early Christians."

"Saints?" Jack asked. "How can they all be saints?"

Chloe laughed. "The meaning of the word saints has changed over time, with the Literalist church reserving the word to describe a very special few … But in Paul's day, all early Christians were referred to as saints, and according to the Dead Sea Scrolls, so were all the Essenes."

Jack playfully punched Punjeeh's arm. "*Saint Punjeeh* … I bet you like that sound of that."

"It does have a nice ring, doesn't it?" Punjeeh laughed.

"Well, St. Punjeeh," Chloe interrupted with a sly grin, "I must warn you that the early Christians and the Essenes had similar ideas about the devil, too."

"Ah-ha," Punjeeh shot back, "I knew there was a catch somewhere."

Chloe chuckled. "You see, Satan was not a central figure in mainstream Judaism two thousand years ago, but the Essenes and the Christians who followed elevated Lucifer's status from that of disobedient angel to the chief perpetrator of all things evil, whose sole purpose was to bring about the demise of humanity."

Much like the notion of guilt and original sin, the devil was a religious concept Jack had difficulty accepting. "You know, I've never really believed in the devil. I've always thought it was just a tool parents used to keep their kids in line."

"I agree with you, my friend. The only devil I've ever seen is inside mankind."

"I think the Gnostics would agree also," Chloe added. "They said that the biblical references about the devil were only symbolic and were instead meant to illustrate the destructive element of man's lower self, or the human ego."

"Saints and Satan. It sounds like these are two words whose meanings have been greatly misunderstood," Punjeeh observed.

"And the Essenes shared other common terminology with the early Christians," Chloe added, "as both groups believed that they were living in the 'End of Days' or 'End Times,' and they both wrote of the coming 'Kingdom of God.' I'm sure you recognize these same pronouncements from your study of Christianity."

"That's more language of St. Paul," Punjeeh noted.

"And not surprisingly, the Gnostics had a much more esoteric understanding of these phrases than their Literalist counterparts," Chloe continued. "They understood the coming 'Kingdom of God' as an allegorical reference to the experience of gnosis, when the ego dissolves and the Gnostic practitioner would realize that all human beings are interconnected, or part of the One Life. For them, The 'Kingdom of God' was not an outer kingdom, but an inner one."

Jack and Punjeeh reflected on Chloe's last statement.

"Their explanation does sound more consistent with the overall theme of Jesus' teachings," Punjeeh offered, "encouraging people to change from within."

"And what about all the End Times stuff?" Jack asked.

"As you probably know, the Literalists understood the End Times or End of Days as referring to the second coming of Jesus, which they believed would signal some sort of Armageddon, or the end of the physical world as we know it.

"But the Gnostics' interpretation was a bit more complicated. They taught that another characteristic of the lower self or ego was its constant need to think about the past and the future, or that the ego was consumed with *time*."

"Come again?" Punjeeh asked. Jack was equally perplexed.

"I told you it was difficult to explain," she warned. "But in short, the Gnostics said that the ego was always directing our thoughts between what has taken place in the past and what may take place in the future."

She waited to let her explanation sink in.

"Think about it for a moment," she continued. "How often are you thinking about and planning what you are going to do in the next five minutes, five hours, or five days? And when you're not thinking about the future, are you remembering the past instead, replaying and reanalyzing it over and over again in your mind?"

"But isn't that human nature?" Jack rebutted.

Chloe laughed. "Sometimes it seems that way, doesn't it? But the Gnostics maintained this was not true human nature, but the nature of the ego instead … and they taught that by constantly directing our thoughts between the past and future, the ego keeps most people from living fully in the present moment."

"That's profound," Punjeeh said thoughtfully.

"And they taught that when the ego dissolves, or when one reaches the state of gnosis, one lives completely in the present moment, free from the mental obsession of past and future."

Jack had listened intently to Chloe's last explanation. "The End of Time," he said.

"Exactly," Chloe replied, happy to see he was grasping another Gnostic concept.

Jack glanced at his watch. He was thinking about the future right now. "How long before we're there, Punj? I want to get hold of that scroll before something happens to it."

"Don't worry, my friend," Punjeeh said. "I have a good feeling about tonight."

# 25

"He's been in there for nearly two hours," Caleb said as they waited on the beach outside the hotel. The sun had begun to set along the western horizon, and the hotel now cast a long shadow over the salty water.

"I hope he didn't get the scroll and take off."

"He won't do that," Youseff replied. "My cousin has a good heart. He's just had a rough life."

"I hope you're right."

Neither spoke as they weighed the possibilities of Tariq's keeping the scroll.

"Maybe we should go inside and look for him," Youseff conceded.

The boys went around front and asked Rasoul for directions to the housekeeping department. Youseff was well aware of the relationship between Tariq and Dalya, and he knew that Tariq would enlist Dalya's help in recovering the lost scroll. They found him sitting at a table in the employee break room, which was adjacent to housekeeping. "What are you doing here?" Tariq asked in a hushed voice. "You're going to get Dalya in trouble."

"What do you care?" Caleb hissed. "Besides … maybe we thought you would run off with the scroll."

Tariq looked at Caleb and smirked. He was about to answer when Dalya entered the room. "You all mustn't be in here. I could get fired."

"I was just telling them that," Tariq assured her.

"Hi, Dalya," Youseff said with puppy-dog eyes. "Sorry about that, we were just leaving."

"Did you find out anything?" Caleb pleaded impatiently.

Dalya reached in the long front pocket of her apron and pulled out the scroll. "Is this what you're looking for?"

Their faces lit up.

"That's it!" Caleb shouted.

Tariq's excitement was quickly replaced with concern. "Dalya, you've got to put it back. I don't want you to be involved like this."

"I'm already involved," she said. "But don't worry, I found it in the trash can. The woman had thrown it away!"

"Whoa," Youseff exclaimed in disbelief, "those Americans are crazy!"

Dalya handed Tariq the scroll. He leaned over and kissed her on the cheek. "Thank you. And I will be in touch soon."

"You must go quickly out the front," Dalya hurried them. "My manager just went out the back door."

\*\*\*

It was dusk by the time Punjeeh's silver BMW reached the driveway leading to the hotel. Jack spotted a large crowd surrounding a lighted pavilion nestled on the hotel beach. Some people looked like they were swaying back and forth to music. Jack pushed the button to lower the rear passenger window and confirmed his speculation. "What's going on?"

"Oh yes," Punjeeh replied. "A very popular Jewish band is playing here tonight."

"I guess so…I bet there're a thousand people over there."

"At least that, I'm sure," Punjeeh said, scanning the crowd. "Their music is quite good. I think you would enjoy it."

Punjeeh slowed the car under the large black awning over the front entrance. Rasoul recognized the vehicle and its occupants as he came out to open their door. "Welcome back to the Château," he said politely.

"Thank you," Punjeeh replied as the three exited the vehicle.

"Did you find your friend?"

"Yes, we did. And she has directed us to your housekeeping department," Punjeeh answered. "Could you tell us where we can find it?"

"Of course, sir. Just go through the lobby, past the restaurant to the first hallway on your right. Follow that all the way 'til it ends, turn left, and housekeeping is down on your right. There is a sign on the door."

"Thank you," Punjeeh replied.

As they walked through the entrance, Jack glanced over at the front desk to see if the manager he had spoken with earlier was still there. But in the process of looking around the room he spotted three young Palestinian boys walking across the lobby toward the beach exit. Jack did a double-take. The boy in front was the one he'd bought the scrolls from!

"That's him!" Jack blurted loudly to Chloe and Punjeeh as he pointed across the busy lobby to Tariq. "The one who sold me the scroll!"

The boys heard the disruption and instinctively turned their heads just in time to see Jack pointing in their direction.

"Let's go!" Tariq yelled to Caleb and Youseff, who bolted out the beach-side exit and headed for the large crowd around the pavilion.

"Wait!" Jack yelled as he darted after them. Punjeeh and Chloe were close behind. He reached the door just in time to see them disappear into the mass of people.

"Was that him?" Punjeeh panted.

"Yes," Jack replied. "I'm sure of it. He ran into the crowd with two of his friends."

"Why did they run away?" Chloe asked.

"I don't know, but I'd sure like to find out where they got the scrolls from."

Jack scanned the throng, which made a large semicircle around the pavilion stage. Now closer, he could see that the crowd was much bigger than it looked from the road.

"Punjeeh, let's split up. You enter over there on the right and I'll take the left. We'll work our way toward the center."

"Okay."

"Chloe, you stay at this vantage point and keep your eyes peeled in case they exit the crowd once we're in the middle."

"Got it."

The boys' height made it easy for them to disappear among the adults. They skillfully maneuvered their way between the clusters of perturbed partygoers who mostly glared at them, as if they were inappropriately trying to get closer to the music. Once they reached what felt like the center, Tariq stopped, motioning the other boys to kneel down.

"That was close," he said.

"They must have seen us come in here," Caleb replied.

"If we work our way toward the stage, maybe we can slip out one of the sides. It's dark enough now they won't be able to see us once we're outside of these lights. Then we'll run toward the water and follow the beach until we're well out of sight. Okay?"

"Okay," they said in unison.

Tariq raised his head and looked around, making sure that the American and his friends were nowhere in sight. They slowly began pushing their way through the groups of listeners in single-file fashion. Tariq, in the lead, suddenly came to a dead stop, causing Caleb and Youseff to bump into him from behind.

"What? Do you see them?" Caleb asked.

Tariq didn't respond.

"What is it?" Caleb repeated.

When Tariq turned around the boys were startled, as his face portrayed a rage they had never seen before. "Look over there," he said.

The boys peered around him and saw Abu, the mentally impaired boy from their village who had been sweeping the porch at the old man's curio shop that morning. He was wearing an oversized long-sleeved shirt and was swaying back and forth awkwardly to the music.

"So what?" Youseff cried. "Maybe he likes Jewish music. The guy doesn't have much up here." He tapped his temple with his index finger.

Tariq looked again at Abu and then turned back to them, his eyes burning. "It's awfully hot for long sleeves, don't you think?" He shook his head in disgust. "That old fucking bastard. People like him choose the helpless to do their dirty work."

Just as Tariq finished speaking, Abu spotted the boys. His eyes were glassy, a combined look of bewilderment and fear etched on his face. He slowly raised one hand as a warning not to come any closer.

"Oh God," Caleb exclaimed as he realized what was happening, "we've got to get away from him."

With their focus shifted toward Abu, the boys didn't realize that Jack had walked up right behind them. He reached his hand out and touched Tariq's shoulder. "I just want to talk to you," he yelled out over the music.

Tariq turned around and looked at him with solemn intensity. Jack realized in an instant that Tariq was not the naïve boy he had portrayed himself to be on the beach the day before. "Get these two away from here," Tariq ordered Jack as he quickly took the scroll out of his back pocket and thrust it into Caleb's belly.

Jack intuitively knew that something bad was about to happen.

Tariq turned and headed quickly toward Abu, pushing the other concert goers aside as he made his way forward. "Get back!" he yelled. "Bomb!"

The lady closest to them screamed. People heard the bomb warning and dispersed in all directions. Jack grabbed Caleb and Youseff and pulled them in front of him. "Run!" he yelled, keeping himself between the boys and Tariq as they ran back toward the hotel.

Tariq reached Abu and hit him chest to chest, wrapping his arms around him and riding him down to the sand.

"Allahu akbar!" Abu cried out as their bodies hit the ground. "God is great."

Seconds later, the bomb went off.

***

Chaos erupted across the beach. Punjeeh heard the blast and immediately went into action. He ran against the flow of people toward the small cloud of smoke that was wafting up from a spot in the sand about a hundred feet in front of him.

When he arrived, he saw the remains of two young men. He quickly scanned the area around the blast site for other casualties and was surprised to see none. As he got closer, he recognized one of the victims as the young man whom Jack had purchased the scroll from a day earlier.

Tears welled up in his eyes.

*Two more young boys are dead, and for what?*

Punjeeh stood silently for a few seconds until the sounds of sirens in the distance woke him from his trance. He headed back to the hotel to see if anyone needed medical attention.

Another day in the Holy Land had come to an end.

✓

# 26

Jack got to know Youseff and Caleb quite well in the days after the bombing, as he and Punjeeh visited their village daily for the next week, attended Tariq and Abu's funeral, and did everything they could to help those affected by the tragic situation.

Fortunately, Jack had been able to recount what he witnessed on the beach to the Israeli authorities, thereby absolving Youseff and Caleb of any suspicion. By the time the police arrived at the curio shop in Medina to apprehend the old man, he had all but disappeared. People in the village were split as to whether he had fled the country or was whisked away by the Israeli Secret Service.

As for the boys, once they realized that Jack and Punjeeh wanted only to help, they explained how they found the scrolls, Tariq's involvement, and their success in reclaiming one thanks to Dalya. Upon hearing their story, Jack promptly provided each boy's family with one thousand dollars, the amount they had originally hoped to get for the scrolls.

The University also planned an archaeological excavation in the coming weeks at the site where the scrolls were found, in the limestone hills near the boys' village of Medina.

Dalya was devastated by Tariq's death, and to add insult to injury, she was fired from her job once hotel management learned of her involvement in recovering the second scroll.

Youseff informed Punjeeh and Jack about her situation. Youseff also explained that Dalya had recently applied for admittance to the pre-med program at the local university. Punjeeh contacted the admissions board, and her application was immediately accepted. He also arranged a spot for her in the hospital's paid internship program the following semester.

Jack hadn't seen much of Chloe since that day. Although she was initially shaken by the blast on the beach, she had recovered quickly in order to help Punjeeh and Jack keep everyone calm until the authorities arrived. But neither he nor Punjeeh had spoken with her since they dropped the second scroll off at her office a few days later.

Now Jack's vacation was coming to a close. He and Punjeeh sat down in the living room with Esther one evening after returning from the boys' village. Esther, always a lover of classical music, pushed Play on her CD player and the uplifting harmony of the *William Tell Overture* filled the room. She lowered the volume slightly so they could converse.

"How were the boys today?" she asked Jack.

"They seem to be doing better," Jack replied. "I think they are pretty resilient kids."

"I agree," Punjeeh concurred. "They are very saddened by what happened, but I gather that it really changed their view of Tariq. I think before they didn't like him very much, and now they see him in a whole new light."

"It's been a real pleasure getting to know them and their families," Jack added. "Between the boys and Chloe, I've experienced things on this trip I never would have otherwise."

"Ahhh," Esther said with a look of remembrance on her face, "speaking of Chloe – she left a message on our answering machine today saying she wanted you two to come by tomorrow around lunchtime."

Jack was relieved to hear she had called. "Great!"

# 27

They found Chloe busy working, open books and papers strewn across her desk. She looked up as Jack and Punjeeh approached her doorway. "Come in," she said, waving them inside and motioning for them to sit down.

"How have you been?" Jack asked as he took the same seat he occupied the last time they were there.

"Better now, I think...that was quite an ordeal."

"You can say that again," Punjeeh added, "and it would have been much worse if not for our young friend."

"Oh yes," Chloe agreed. "He was our savior, wasn't he?"

Jack's thoughts went to Tariq and the fateful night on the beach.

"He was quite a brave kid," Punjeeh added. "And if you think about it, had he not stolen the scrolls from the other boys and sold them to us, he probably wouldn't have been on the beach that night, and many more people would have died...so sometimes, even a seemingly inappropriate action can, in fact, be part of the universe's master plan."

Jack pondered the ramifications of what Punjeeh said for a moment, then turned back to Chloe. "Well, I'm glad to see you again," he grinned. "I was beginning to think you didn't like me anymore."

"Oh, Jack," Chloe replied, shaking her head in a way that assured him his fear wasn't justified. "This scroll took a little longer to translate than the first one, and I wanted to double-check everything to make sure it was correct before I shared it with you."

"And what does it say?" Punjeeh asked excitedly.

"As we suspected, the First Secret Mystery provides a lot of insight about how the Gnostics viewed Jesus' crucifixion and resurrection," she replied.

"That's fantastic!" Jack exclaimed. "Let's have a look!"

Chloe hedged. "I think I should make some prefatory remarks before you do," she said and paused. "I have a confession to make. I haven't been completely honest with you about something."

Jack's ears perked up. For once he was not the one surprised in a conversation with these two. In the back of his mind, he had always thought that Chloe was hiding something. "And what might that be?" he asked calmly.

Chloe grimaced. "Remember how I told you that all the stories surrounding Jesus' birth and many of the miracles he is believed to have performed appeared in older Greek and Roman religious traditions?"

Jack's mind raced with possibilities. Had Chloe not been honest about *that*? Had she exaggerated or even fabricated parts? "You're not going to tell us that those things aren't true, are you?" his voice faltered.

Chloe wrinkled her nose. "No, Jack." She was surprised by his question. "In fact, it's just the opposite. What I didn't tell you was that the virgin birth, the miracles and the like, those things are just the tip of the iceberg. They are only the *beginning* of the similarities between the stories told about Jesus and the gods of the Greek and Roman Mystery religions."

Jack's mind came to a screeching halt. He felt a lump forming in the back of his throat. For some reason, it had never occurred to him that there may be more similarities than the ones Chloe had already shared with them.

Punjeeh was equally perplexed. "My dear Chloe, why would you think you couldn't tell us everything?" he smiled good-naturedly. "And what on earth are these Mystery religions you just mentioned?"

Chloe answered cautiously. "I'm sorry, Punjeeh…but based on our conversations at Bethlehem, I just wasn't sure if the two of you could handle any more information."

Jack assumed immediately that she was really referring to just him.

"But before you read the second scroll, if it's going to make any sense to you, then you'll need to know certain things …" she added.

Jack felt the lump in his throat dissipate. Whatever she had to say, he wanted to hear it. "Don't edit yourself on my account."

Professor King's entrance broke the tension in the air.

"Sorry I'm late," he said, hustling in, clutching an overstuffed satchel to his chest. "I brought the things you asked for, Chloe."

Jack and Punjeeh stood up to greet him. "Hello, Professor," Jack said, extending his hand.

"Good day, gentlemen, and congratulations on your acquisition of the second scroll, although I was dreadfully sorry to hear about the unfortunate incident you went through in the process."

"Oh, we're fine," Jack replied. "Thanks to a young man named Tariq Muhammad."

"Yes, of course," Professor King replied. "I wish this country had a thousand more with his qualities."

"I'm sure we do," said Punjeeh, "but hopefully one day soon, such heroics will not be necessary."

"Let's hope not," Professor King agreed.

"You're just in time, Professor," Chloe continued. "Punjeeh has asked me to explain the Greco-Roman Mystery religions."

"Ah-ha," Professor King replied with enthusiasm, "perhaps the most interesting religious movement in antiquity!" Chloe winked at Jack and Punjeeh. She well knew Professor King's love for the Mystery religions.

"It is my humble opinion that these ancient spiritual movements provided the building blocks for Christianity," the professor added. His remark elicited raised eyebrows from Jack and Punjeeh. "But do forgive my interruption, Chloe. Please continue." He took a seat to the side of Chloe's desk as Jack and Punjeeh sat back down.

Chloe waited for them to get situated before starting. "Before I say anything about the Mystery religions, perhaps we should revisit the religious climate of the ancient world. It's important to remember that the ancients had very different ideas about religion and God than we do in modern times.

"If you remember from our conversation in Bethlehem," she continued, "Zeus, Jupiter, and most of the other gods of the Roman Empire were quite different in temperament from the loving God most people believe in today. These ancient gods were seen as cold and uncaring masters who had little concern about the day-to-day affairs of the average man or woman. They symbolized power, and that power was to be feared. The ancients labored through sacrifice and offerings in order to appease them, hoping primarily to avoid their wrath."

"The image of God that is prevalent in today's society," Professor King added, "that of a comforting and forgiving father figure, was practically nonexistent in the ancient world."

"It sounds like Zeus and Jupiter were similar in that way to Jehovah from the Old Testament," Punjeeh noted.

"An excellent observation, Dr. Punjeeh," Professor King said enthusiastically. "Jehovah, the Jewish god of the Old Testament, is often portrayed as a jealous and angry god who destroys whole cities, punishes his followers for their transgressions, and demands worship and sacrifices be made in his honor. In this way, Jehovah's behavior was consistent with the other prevalent gods of Greece and Rome during that period."

"These ideas about religion had remained static for hundreds of years," Chloe said, picking up where she had stopped. "But in the centuries just before the rise of Christianity, religious thinking in the ancient world began to change, and those changes are best exemplified in the practices and beliefs of what were called the Mystery religions."

Chloe drew a deep breath.

"You see, the gods of the Mystery religions brought a new element to religious practices in the ancient world. Unlike Zeus, Jupiter, or even Jehovah, the gods of the Mystery religions were portrayed as *all-loving deities, who cared about the lives of everyday people*. Their followers would pray to them in times of difficulty, for comfort and support, not just out of fear of retribution.

"And unlike the traditional religions of Greece and Rome, the gods of the Mystery religions offered its adherents a way to experience peace and happiness in this life, and a heavenly reward in the next ... because it wasn't until the emergence of the Mystery religions that the idea of a positive afterlife really took hold."

The inference from Chloe's last statement elicited a question from Jack. "So are you saying that before these Mystery religions, people didn't believe in heaven?"

"For the most part, no," she replied. "Even ancient Judaism didn't believe there was a heaven. Jehovah of the Old Testament offered no such thing."

As usual, Professor King couldn't resist the urge to add to Chloe's explanation. "What my dear Chloe is saying, gentlemen, is that the Mystery religions *spearheaded an evolution in peoples' thinking about God,* as it was here the notion first emerged in Greek and Roman thought that God could be a completely benevolent being, all-loving and forgiving, and that he wanted a personal relationship with human beings."

"Those are Christian ideals I have taken for granted my whole life," Jack commented.

"That's correct," Professor King offered, "but if you had lived in the ancient world–that is, prior to the advent of the Mystery religions–this would not have been the case. I often point out to my students that with the advent of the Mystery religions, either God changed … or our *ideas* about God changed."

Something about Professor King's statement resonated deeply within Jack. *Did God change? Or did we change?*

"Many of these Mystery religion gods we've already discussed," Chloe continued. "There was Dionysus, Osiris, Adonis, Mithras, and a handful of others, but the stories told about them and their teachings were very similar."

Punjeeh thought for a moment. "And if memory serves me correctly, didn't you say it was the stories of these gods that the gospel writers borrowed from when they wrote of Jesus' virgin birth and the miracles he performed?"

Chloe looked at him with a knowing smile. "Bingo."

A look of realization swept across Punjeeh's face. "So it's no wonder that Professor King referred to the Mystery religions as the building blocks of Christianity. Their benevolent ideas about God, the stories of the virgin birth and the miracles, it all sounds like the beliefs espoused by the early Christians."

"Quite right, Dr. Punjeeh," Professor King added. "From a theological standpoint, Jesus and the gods of the Mystery religions were in full agreement. Their teachings of love and forgiveness, the virgin births, and the miracles ascribed to them were virtually identical. I believe that the average person living in antiquity would have viewed Jesus as a Jewish version of a Mystery religion god, because the similarities between early Christianity and the Mystery religions are, quite simply, undeniable."

Something still puzzled Jack. "So why were they called Mystery religions?"

"Good question, Jack," Chloe answered with a smile. "They were referred to as Mystery religions because the initiates of these sects were said to go through various stages, or levels, where they were taught secret teachings that they referred to as *the secret mysteries.* Consequently, the religions themselves became known as the Mystery religions."

"Just like the Secret Mystery mentioned in the scroll," Jack emphasized.

"Exactly! Like the Gnostics that followed them, adherents of the Mystery religions taught that the ultimate aim of their followers was to experience a mystical union with God directly."

"Gnosis!" Punjeeh exclaimed and then scratched his brow for a moment. "But whatever happened to these Mystery religions?"

"That's an easy one," Chloe quipped. "They met the same fate as the Gnostics. After the Emperor Constantine joined forces with the Literalist Christian Church, it wasn't long before the Mystery religions, the Gnostics, and all the older Greek and Roman religious traditions were declared illegal. Within a few generations, almost all of their followers were killed and their writings systematically destroyed. Before long, there was hardly a trace of them left."

"Amazing," Punjeeh said, shaking his head.

Jack sensed there was more. "So is that it?" he asked, studying Chloe's face for confirmation. "I mean, that's interesting stuff, but you said a minute ago that the similarities we discussed last week were just the beginning."

Chloe slowly leaned back in her chair and bit her lower lip. "Yes, Jack, I'm afraid there's more I need to tell you."

Her tone caused the lump in the back of Jack's throat to reappear.

"In addition to what you already know about the virgin birth and miracle stories," she began, "many of the Mystery religions had sacred communion rituals, which encouraged their followers to consume *the body and blood* of the Mystery religion god."

Jack and Punjeeh remembered all the times in church they had taken communion.

"For example, the Greek god Dionysus was recognized as the god of wine, and his companion and lover Demeter was the goddess of bread or grain. Followers of the Mystery religions performed a sacred ceremony where they 'ate the body' and 'drank the blood' of these gods in order to become one with them. This ancient communion tradition predates Christianity by hundreds of years."

"And the followers of the Mystery religion of Mithras had a very similar ritual," Professor King added. "After slaughtering a sacrificial bull, the high priest would speak these very words at their version of the communion ceremony, and I quote:

*'He who will not eat of my body and drink of my blood, so that he will be made one with me and I with him, he shall not know salvation.'"*

Jack and Punjeeh's astonished faces silenced Professor King.

Punjeeh was the first to comment. "This is yet another unbelievable revelation. I had always wondered why Jesus chose wine and bread as symbols for his body and blood."

"Now you know," Professor King responded. "It was a carry-over from the rituals of the Mystery religions."

Chloe paused momentarily. "But I'm afraid even the communion ceremony is not the most striking parallel between Christianity and the Mystery religions—and there is no easy way to say this—the amazing truth is that *all the gods of the Mystery religions were sacrificed for the sins of their followers, only to be resurrected a few days later, thus confirming their divinity and ultimate power over death.*"

"Oh my God," Punjeeh exclaimed as he leaned back in his chair and put his hand on his forehead.

"For instance, Dionysus was unjustly killed by his enemies, but defied his fate by rising to life again, he then appeared to his amazed disciples before ascending into heaven, and the whole chain of events was acted out regularly before Mystery religion initiates in what they called a 'passion play.'"

"Likewise, Adonis and Mithras were both put to death for the sins of mankind, but they too were resurrected shortly thereafter. Their stories were commemorated every spring, in celebrations that were very similar to our modern-day Easter."

Professor King couldn't resist the temptation to add to her explanation. "Another notable quality of these Mystery gods were the titles bestowed upon them by their adherents. Since the Mystery religions taught that their gods had been a sacrifice for the sins of humanity, these gods were given titles such as *the only begotten son, the divine savior, the sin bearer,* and *the redeemer.*"

"All phrases used to describe Jesus," Punjeeh said in disbelief.

Professor King agreed. "And in another linguistic parallel, Bacchus, the virgin-born, dying, and resurrecting god of the Roman Mystery religions, was said to have spoken the following words centuries before the Christian movement began:

> 'It is I who guides you, it is I who protects you, it is I who saves you, it is I who am Alpha and Omega.'

"Words that were also offered by Jesus in the Book of Revelation."

"And in a seemingly trivial similarity," Chloe added, "Dionysus was said to have ridden on the back of a donkey into the city of Athens when it was his time to die."

"Just as Jesus rode a donkey into Jerusalem when he was to be crucified," Punjeeh muttered.

"Correct," Chloe answered. "But the similarity proved not to be trivial after all, because in the Mystery religions, the donkey was a symbol of the lower self, the ego. And the Mystery god's decision to ride a donkey to his death was understood to be a symbol of his victory over his lower nature."

Chloe turned to Professor King. "Can we see the picture I asked you to bring?"

"It's right here." He reached into his satchel and laid a photo on the desk. It was a snapshot of an ancient stone tablet. Carved into the tablet was the image of a man hung on a cross. Greek letters surrounded the image.

"What do you see?" she asked Jack and Punjeeh as she pointed down at the photo.

"Christ crucified," Punjeeh replied cautiously.

Chloe smiled understandingly. "This is one of the oldest known depictions of a crucifixion, but despite the obvious similarity, it's not Jesus Christ. The inscription on it is written in Greek and states that this carving depicts the crucifixion of Orpheus Bacchus, a prophet of the Mystery religion god Dionysus."

"Unbelievable," Punjeeh exhaled as he studied the photo in front of him.

"But it could just as easily have been an image of Prometheus," Professor King interjected, "for he too was killed for the sake of mankind by being *nailed up with his arms extended ...*" He abruptly held out his arms, mimicking the crucifixion position. "And let us not forget to mention Attis, the Mystery god of Asia Minor who was put to death as a sacrifice for mankind by being *hung on a tree.*"

The statement struck a chord with Punjeeh. "*Cursed is everyone who is hung on a tree,*" he said aloud.

Jack looked over at him. "What did you say?"

"St. Paul's letter to the Galatians," Punjeeh replied slowly. "In Jesus' day, being crucified was often referred to as being *hung on a tree.*"

"Bravo, Dr. Punjeeh, bravo," Professor King said, once again impressed by Punjeeh's knowledge of the Bible. "And we could go on and on with these examples, gentlemen."

"I know this may seem too unbelievable to be true," Chloe spoke up, "but the fact of the matter is, the story of the sacrificial death and resurrection of the son of God is not original to Christianity."

Jack and Punjeeh stared at the photo of the ancient crucifixion while Chloe and Professor King awaited their response. Punjeeh was the first to break the silence. "What you speak of are the hallmarks of Christianity, Chloe," he said in a way that made it clear even he was disturbed by the latest revelation. "And what may I ask exactly are you implying? That Jesus was not crucified under Pontius Pilate, and that the resurrection never took place? That it was just another story borrowed from these Mystery religions?"

Chloe leaned forward and looked Punjeeh square in the eye. "Yes. I believe that is an argument worthy of serious consideration."

Punjeeh sank back into his chair. "But that's ridiculous," he blurted out, visibly shaken. "It is one of the most well-known events in human history! How could it be possible that it never happened?"

Professor King reached into his satchel and pulled out another textbook. "Perhaps it would be helpful if you read what one of the founding fathers of Literalist Christianity, St. Justin the Martyr, had to say about the similarities between Jesus and the gods of the Mystery religions."

He thumbed through the pages and then sat the open book down on the desk in front of Jack and Punjeeh. "St. Justin wrote this letter to some Roman officials when he was arguing for the acceptance of the growing Christian religion, and this paragraph is particularly telling of his knowledge regarding the similarities between Jesus and the gods of the Mystery religions.

'And when we say also that Jesus, who is the first-birth of God, was produced without sexual union, and that He, our Teacher, was crucified and died, and rose again, and ascended into heaven, *we propound nothing different from what you believe regarding the gods you worship, sons of Jupiter and Zeus.*'

"Remember that Jupiter and Zeus were the major gods of the Roman Empire," Professor King explained. "All of the Mystery gods–Dionysus, Mithras, Prometheus, and the like–were said to have been born from a mortal woman, a virgin, but their father was supposed to have been Jupiter or Zeus himself...just as the Literalist church taught that Jesus was born of the Virgin Mary but was said to be the son of Jehovah, the god of the Jews."

Punjeeh stared at the verse in front of him. "So the early Literalist church knew of these similarities?" he asked incredulously.

"Absolutely!" Professor King barked. "And they readily admitted them!"

"But how could they explain these repetitions to their followers?"

"Simple, Dr. Punjeeh," Professor King replied quickly, "They blamed the devil!"

Jack and Punjeeh looked at him blankly.

"I know this will be hard to believe," Chloe offered, "but the early Literalist church fathers claimed the devil had created and distributed the stories of the Mystery religion gods several hundred years in advance of Jesus' coming as part of a preemptive effort to discredit the historical truth of Christianity ... and they even coined an official name for it: *diabolical mimicry.*"

Professor King laughed. "Yes, gentlemen, as illogical as it sounds, the position of the Literalist church was simply this: the older stories about the virgin-born, miracle-performing, dying and resurrecting gods of the Mystery religions were fictitious creations of the devil, but all stories about Jesus were to be believed as undeniable historical events."

Punjeeh was stunned. "That's the most ridiculous reasoning I've ever heard!"

"I couldn't agree more," Professor King replied, "but believe it or not, even today many educated church leaders who are familiar with the similarities between Christianity and the Mystery religions still invoke the theological argument of diabolical mimicry as their best defense!"

"But if people knew this, I think everything would change," Punjeeh argued.

"Would it?" Chloe asked rhetorically. "I'm afraid that the few Christian pastors over the past few years that have been brave enough to advocate discarding these outdated beliefs and focusing only on the revolutionary aspect of Jesus' teachings have been largely ignored."

Professor King's expression turned solemn. "Sadly, that is correct, gentlemen, because in most Christian denominations today, the beauty of Jesus' message is still overshadowed by people's need to *believe* in supernatural tales about his life and death."

Punjeeh closed his eyes as he digested this new information. His face exhibited a look of profound contemplation. Finally, he spoke. "My dear Chloe, I am sorry for my earlier outburst. It seems as though you found a belief so deep in me that even I did not realize how ingrained it was."

Punjeeh leaned back in his chair. Chloe was relieved to see his usual relaxed nature begin to return. She now turned her attention to Jack, who had been uncharacteristically reserved throughout the last part of the conversation.

"Jack?" she asked hesitantly. "What do you think of all this?"

Jack waited a second before answering. "In a way," he said slowly, "the whole thing makes more sense now."

Punjeeh sat back up in his chair. He couldn't decide which was more shocking—Chloe's revelations or Jack's last remark. "Could you please explain yourself, my friend?"

"Well, I never did understand the reason why God would need to sacrifice his own son to save us … it just never did add up. I mean, if God is really God, an all-powerful being, why would he need to do that? If we needed forgiveness, couldn't he just forgive us?" Jack paused again. "But if the whole crucifixion thing was just a story somebody made up, and it was not to be taken, uh … *literally*, I guess God is off the hook in my book."

"Well put, Jack," Professor King answered enthusiastically. "My sentiments exactly."

Punjeeh placed his hand on Jack's shoulder. "My God, man … you never cease to amaze me."

"The only thing I don't understand is," Jack continued, "why would they come up with a story like that? 'God's son is sacrificed for the sins of the world.' It's just bizarre."

"That's another excellent point," Chloe resumed. "But try to understand that the story of a dying and resurrecting son of God, one who is sacrificed for the sins of the world, was very appropriate for the time in human history. It would have had special significance in the lives of the ancients that would be hard to understand today."

"What do you mean?" Jack asked.

"Keep in mind that life was very difficult in antiquity. Infant mortality rates were high, there was no modern medicine, and death by starvation was a real possibility. In addition, the vast majority of the people were either oppressed or enslaved – ruled by a privileged minority."

"It's difficult for modern man to grasp the hardships the ancient peoples lived with," Professor King added.

"And not unlike today," Chloe continued, "the circumstances under which people lived were explained in the context of their religion. But the key difference between then and now is that in the ancient world, the gods were not considered a friend of man. In fact, most people believed that the gods *were the cause* of the bad things that happened to them, not the solution, and the only way the ancients thought they could appease the gods and avoid their wrath was to offer them sacrifices."

"Ritual sacrifice was very much a part of the ancient religious landscape," Professor King clarified. "Animals were regularly offered to the gods of Greece and Rome in hopes to gain favor and avoid misfortune. As we discussed earlier, even Jehovah of the Old Testament required such rituals."

"And to add to their dilemma, most people in the ancient world maintained a deeply held belief that man was guilty of an *original sin*," Chloe added, "that he was responsible to God for the faults and mistakes of his ancestors."

"Like Adam and Eve, and their fall from the Garden of Eden," Jack concluded.

"That's right, Jack," Professor King encouraged him, "the Judaic story in the Old Testament conveys the idea of original sin very well, but the other religions of antiquity had similar stories that expressed the same belief."

"And that's why the Mystery religions were so revolutionary for the time period," Chloe continued. "Through their stories they conveyed a very powerful message: God has changed, there is a new covenant; He has forgiven all man's transgressions and absolved his original sin. From now on, God promises he will no longer behave like a tyrannical master but will be a loving father instead.

"And to prove his sincerity to the ancients, God offered his only begotten son to be sacrificed for the sins of the world, to be the last and final sacrifice—and the resurrection was offered as proof that there was life after death, something most people in the ancient world didn't believe in."

"Yes, gentlemen," Professor King concluded, "Christianity and the other Mystery religions marked a profound shift in our beliefs and ideas about God. Man's view of God changed from that of a powerful yet uncaring master into a loving and protecting father figure, and furthermore, it was here in which the belief in a heavenly afterlife really took hold in man's psyche. In my humble opinion, the beliefs espoused by the Mystery religions and early Christianity were the next logical step in the evolution of human spiritual development."

Jack and Punjeeh sat in silent reflection.

"It's the best explanation I've ever heard," Jack said, "but sacrificing your son still seems like a bizarre way to get your point across."

Professor King let out a loud laugh. "I agree, Jack, to modern man it would ... but this was the ancient world, and for them the message was timely."

# 28

Jack sat in a stupor and gazed across the desk at Chloe. He came to Jerusalem with the intention of re-kindling the Christian faith of his childhood, but instead, Chloe and Professor King had turned his understanding of Christian history and ideology upside down.

But surprisingly, he was okay with it.

Their explanations resolved the two elements of traditional church teachings he never understood: fear and guilt.

*God didn't send his only son to die for our sins—what a frickin relief*, he thought to himself.

And as Chloe had pointed out on several occasions, the absence of supernatural events did nothing to negate the beauty of Jesus' message. If anything, the new revelations had demonstrated to him that the essence of Christianity's teachings delved deeper into the nature of spirituality than he had previously imagined.

Now he wanted to know more.

"What's the First Secret Mystery?" Jack asked. "Can we see the translation now?"

"Of course," Chloe replied.

She opened the top drawer of her desk and pulled out a sheet of paper. Jack immediately recognized her handwriting.

"Okay … here's the translation." She laid it on the desk in front of them. "As I mentioned, the First Secret Mystery is about the crucifixion and resurrection."

Jack and Punjeeh peered down and read the following:

*Since the persecution of so many brothers and sisters in gnosis, I'm afraid I may be the only one left who knows the meaning of the First Secret Mystery, or the truth behind the crucifixion and the resurrection. So despite the oath I took to secrecy, I now believe I must divulge its essence.*

*Therefore, the truth of the First Secret Mystery is this: The crucifixion and resurrection are but a story, a metaphor. The crucifixion represents the death of the Lower Self, and the resurrection symbolizes the Eternal Nature of the Higher Self.*

*The lower self, or ego, is the part of us that fights, that condemns, and mistakenly believes itself to be a distinct entity, separate from all other living things. But this idea of separateness is an illusion, and the ego's constant adherence to this flawed way of thinking produces all human suffering.*

*The higher self, or spirit, is the part of us that loves, that forgives, and is in a constant state of peace. This Spirit is our Divine Spark, or the part of the One Eternal Life that is inside each one of us. Our higher self knows the perennial truth: We are all One.*

*So with human beings, it is only the ego that can die. And it is through the example of Jesus on the Cross that we are shown how the ego dies.*

*Because the ego cannot be killed by fighting or struggle ... on the contrary, the ego is strengthened through fighting and struggle.*

*The ego will only succumb through acceptance, and it dies every time we completely and totally accept the present moment. If we allow the present moment to be as it is, in whatever form it takes, then the ego no longer has power over us.*

*This is the deepest meaning imparted to us through the image of Jesus on the cross: acceptance of everything, even the seemingly unacceptable.*

*May the revealing of this First Secret Mystery guide you farther along the path to gnosis, and I leave you with the question posed to us by the Apostle:*

*"Don't you know that you are the temple of God?"*

*St. Paul's Letter to the Corinthians 3:16.*

"Wow," Jack said after reading the scroll. "That was deep. I'm not sure I understand it all, but it was deep."

Punjeeh was equally impressed. "That's one of the most beautiful things I've ever read."

"It certainly confirms what many scholars have suspected about the Gnostics for some time," Professor King said. "Namely, that they did not view the crucifixion and resurrection as a historical event, but rather as a spiritual allegory, designed to impart a deeper meaning to those on the path to gnosis."

"And this scroll brings forth the hidden meaning in that allegory," Chloe added. "The crucifixion was a symbol for the death of the ego, or the lower self, and it's clear from this writing that for the Gnostics, the crucifixion was also a symbol of how the ego can be destroyed."

"That's the part I don't understand," Jack interrupted. "How is the crucifixion a symbol for that?"

"Because for the Gnostics, the image of Jesus on the cross was the archetype of acceptance," she answered, "and they maintained that total and complete acceptance of the present moment was the path to ego destruction."

"Look at it this way," Professor King offered for clarification. "Most people would agree, especially in those days, that crucifixion was one of the most horrible fates one could suffer. Yet by this time in the gospel story, the reader knows Jesus had several opportunities to avoid this fate. But for some reason, he doesn't, and the question is, Why?"

"We were always taught that it was because Jesus needed to die for our sins," Punjeeh answered, "that he had to sacrifice himself in order to save us."

"That's the Literalist interpretation," Professor King replied, "and now we have proof that the Gnostics understood it differently. They saw Jesus on the cross as a symbol for the death of the ego, and this image was designed to impart the idea that the ego won't be destroyed through fighting or struggle, but only when we totally and completely accept life on life's terms."

"In a way it is so simple," Punjeeh enunciated slowly, "but so true."

"And in my personal experience," Professor King replied, "it is something that is very difficult for human beings to put into practice."

Something inside Jack disagreed. "But if we accept life on life's terms, would anything ever change? What about all the injustices in the world? Do we just accept those, too?"

"Ah, my dear Jack," Professor King offered thoughtfully, "you raise a good point, but I think you are confusing internal and external acceptance. In other words, undoubtedly the Gnostics would encourage taking external action to change things when change is possible, but what about those situations where nothing can be done?"

"Like the rain," Punjeeh mused, referencing their prior conversation.

"Exactly," Professor King proclaimed. "The point of the Gnostic teaching is this: Can you internally accept a situation that is beyond your control?"

"I can see what you're saying now," Jack conceded. "Jesus on the cross—a symbol for internal acceptance of whatever life brings."

Professor King smiled heartily. "I applaud you, Mr. Jack, as most Christians can't see the deeper meaning in the crucifixion story, for they have been too long indoctrinated with Literalist beliefs."

Jack's epiphany grew. "So the crucifixion itself was a parable, a story, designed to convey this deeper meaning of the death of the ego through acceptance."

Chloe's eyes twinkled. She was thrilled at his perception. "Very good, Jack, and yes, the crucifixion was a parable…or more accurately, a parable among parables. As Jesus taught only in parables, in some ways it's not surprising that the most significant event ascribed to his life was a parable as well."

Punjeeh sank back in his chair. "Amazing …just utterly amazing."

# 29

It was in that moment that the strangest of thoughts occurred to Jack, and it was so strange he almost dared not utter it. But once the thought had emerged, it formed a question that had to be asked. He reached across the desk and grabbed Chloe's hand, his voice becoming deadly serious. "If the virgin birth, the miracles, the communion ceremony, the crucifixion, and the resurrection were all borrowed stories from these Mystery religions, and all of their gods were mythical, how do we know that Jesus isn't a mythical god, too?"

Punjeeh looked over at Jack, his eyes growing wide as saucers. "My God, man!" he stammered, "You're right! If we remove those stories, what can we say that we actually know about the life of Jesus?"

Now it was Chloe and Professor King's turn to be surprised.

"That's very insightful, Jack," Chloe concurred, and looked to Professor King to answer.

"Bravo, gentlemen," Professor King said. "Bravo. That is an excellent question, and one that very few scholars have the courage or self-awareness to even ask. And based on all the evidence, or should I say lack of evidence, it's a very reasonable one. How can we be sure that a man named Jesus actually existed? And while no one can offer a definitive answer, I would be happy to share with you the three most prominent scholarly views."

"Please do," Punjeeh responded quickly.

Professor King cleared his throat and began. "The first argument is the orthodox position. It states that everything Chloe and I have told you is a complete misinterpretation of the facts. That despite the obvious similarities to the Mystery religions, Jesus of Nazareth was in fact born of a virgin, performed miracles, was crucified under Pontius

Pilate, and rose from the dead three days later. He then dispatched his disciples to carry his message around the world, and ascended to heaven shortly thereafter. The fact that virtually identical stories were attributed to the Mystery religion gods centuries before the advent of Christianity is either one of the most amazing coincidences of all time, or a shrewd plot hatched by the devil hundreds of years in advance, all in a *diabolical* effort to deceive humanity ... In other words, perhaps the Literalist church got it right."

As crazy as this version of the truth now sounded, Jack could still feel a part of him wanting to believe it. It was certainly the easiest thing to do, and perhaps then he could just go home and forget that any of this ever happened. Of course he knew that wasn't realistic, just as he now knew most everything he had been brought up to believe about Jesus wasn't realistic either.

"Scratch that one," he said, "That's not it."

"As you wish," Professor King replied and bowed his head.

"The second position is on the other end of the spectrum, and is that of the skeptic. It recognizes the logic in your question, and argues that if all we know about the life of Jesus are fictitious stories copied from mythical Greek and Roman gods, it is just as likely that Jesus was a mythical god, too. There are many well-respected scholars who argue this position, and they have ample material to work with, the most compelling of which is that there is no contemporary historical record of the life of Jesus of Nazareth other than the biblical gospels themselves."

Jack stopped to think through this possibility. In some ways the theory seemed plausible; however, there was also a strong feeling inside him that said this interpretation of the facts wasn't the correct one either.

"The skeptic's theory has ample holes, Jack," Chloe spoke up, sensing his dilemma. "It's not a necessary step to conclude that Jesus never existed just because legendary stories were told about his life. For instance, I believe the first president of your country, George Washington, was said to have chopped down his father's cherry tree and refused to lie about it, yet his biographer later admitted he created the entire anecdote in an effort to convey the importance of honesty in President Washington's life ... so while people have often made up stories about historical figures, it doesn't mean the figures themselves never existed."

Chloe's reasoning made sense to him. Invented stories about Jesus' life didn't disprove his existence.

Jack turned his attention back to Professor King. "I guess that's a possibility ... But you said there were three main views, so what's the last one?"

Professor King smiled. "The third argument is referred to as the middle path, because it falls somewhere in between the former two. It states that Jesus was a revolutionary Jewish teacher from Judea, who traveled throughout the ancient world spreading his message of love and forgiveness to all who would listen."

"And due to the many similarities between the Jewish Essenes and early Christians," Chloe interrupted, "it's highly likely that Jesus was a member of the Essene sect."

Jack and Punjeeh quickly remembered the coinciding beliefs of the Essenes and the early Christians that Chloe had explained in prior conversations.

"I think the Essene-Christian connection is a fairly easy one to make," Professor King confirmed. "Their shared ideas about the Jewish Messiah, ritualistic bathing, and common religious terminology strongly infer that the first Christians came from the Essene ranks."

"And those who adopt the middle view also agree that it's quite possible Jesus the Essene died an unfortunate death," added Chloe, "perhaps at the hands of the Roman government or other jealous Jewish leaders."

"Such has been the fate of holy men and women since the dawn of eternity," Punjeeh sighed.

"Sadly, I would agree, Dr. Punjeeh," Professor King acknowledged. "But in any case, sometime after Jesus' death, possibly even many years later, his Essene followers began to believe that he had in fact been the long-awaited Jewish Messiah. And when stories about Jesus and his teachings circulated out of Judea and into the Essene communities of the Jewish diaspora, they began to take on new meaning. The Essenes, who had been influenced by the Mystery religions, saw a theological intersection between the revolutionary teachings of this Jewish teacher from Judea and the dying and resurrecting gods of the Mystery religions. And in an attempt to take Jesus' message to a wider audience, namely the Gentiles, these followers glorified the account of Jesus' life by adding in the popular tales attributed to the gods of the Mystery religions."

Something in Jack's gut told him this scenario was closest to the truth, Punjeeh's expression confirmed he was thinking the same thing.

"It does seem more likely that the early Christians would embellish the life of a real spiritual teacher rather than making up someone altogether," Punjeeh observed.

"I must agree," Professor King added. "In my opinion, the first people we would call Christians were men and women of Essene Jewish origin that had been heavily influenced by the ideas and stories of the Greek and Roman Mystery religions. They interpreted the stories about a revolutionary Jewish teacher from Judea in two ways: as the prophesized Jewish Messiah and the allegorical embodiment of the gods of the Mystery religions. So in effect, they merged the two religions, creating a synthesis of sorts, and the result of this synthesis has come down to us in the form of Christianity and the gospels."

Punjeeh wanted further clarification "Are you saying that the first Christians combined the tenets of Essene Judaism with those of the Greek and Roman Mystery religions, and that this combination formed something new, neither exclusively Jewish nor exclusively Greek and Roman?"

"Exactly, Dr. Punjeeh," said Professor King. "Both Essenic Judaism and the Greek and Roman Mystery religions contributed to the formation of Christianity. The Essene practice of cleansing one's sins through water was transformed into the Christian rite of baptism, while the communion ceremony and crucifixion-resurrection had clear origins in the Mystery religions. "

Punjeeh shook his head in amazement. "That's quite a theory."

"It makes sense," Jack agreed. "Something doesn't come from nothing."

"I'm glad you liked the third scenario," Professor King added, "and perhaps you will allow me to present an even more radical extension of it?"

"Professor King, could there be a more radical extension than what I've heard today?" Punjeeh asked sarcastically.

Professor King chuckled. "Touché, Dr. Punjeeh, touché. But I would like to add that some scholars who ascribe to the middle-path theory also point out that the figure I described as Jesus could just as well have been the Essene Teacher of Righteousness!"

"The Teacher of Righteousness from the Dead Sea Scrolls?" Jack asked incredulously. "But I thought Chloe said he lived more than one hundred years before Jesus?"

"Very good, Jack," Chloe responded enthusiastically, happy to see he remembered. "But scholars' only reason to place Jesus later in time was because we know from the Roman record the dates of Pilate's rule. But if Jesus was not crucified under Pilate, he could have lived at a slightly earlier time."

"And let's not forget that the Teacher of Righteousness, like Jesus, was quite a revolutionary for his day," Professor King said. "He led a break from mainstream Judaism, emphasized baptism, and encouraged new and liberal interpretations of the Old Testament. We know from the Dead Sea Scrolls that his Essene followers would hold him in extremely high regard for decades to follow, and that he too suffered a martyr's death at the hands of Pharisaic priests... all things that were later attributed to Jesus."

"Of course!" Punjeeh exclaimed. "I forgot about that!"

Jack was skeptical. "But isn't it just as possible that Jesus was another Essene teacher, and not this Teacher of Righteousness fellow?"

"You are right, Jack," Professor King conceded, "we can't say for sure, and anyone who says they can is really no different in mind-set from the Literalist church. However, there is one more piece of evidence in the Dead Sea Scrolls to suggest that Jesus and the Teacher are one and the same."

Jack and Punjeeh waited eagerly for Professor King to continue.

"Scholars have noted that the language used in the Dead Sea Scrolls to describe the Teacher would have had a certain appeal to those influenced by the Mystery religions, as the scrolls refer to the Teacher as the keeper of God's *secret mysteries*, and that God has hidden his secret mysteries *in the heart of the Teacher of Righteousness!*"

Jack and Punjeeh were dumbfounded.

Professor King stopped and then glanced quickly at his watch. "Gentlemen, I'm sorry, but I am late for class again."

"You're just going to leave us like that?" Jack protested lightheartedly. "I mean, do you really think it's possible that Jesus and the Teacher of Righteousness were one and the same?"

Professor King smiled. "Some things are destined to remain a *mystery*, I'm afraid." He took a small envelope out of his jacket pocket.

"Here is the university's offer to acquire the scrolls," he said as he handed the envelope to Jack. "I hope we can come to an agreement."

"Thank you for everything, Professor," Punjeeh said.

"It was my pleasure," the professor responded. He turned to Chloe. "And thank you, my dear Chloe, for introducing me to these fine gentlemen."

Chloe smiled warmly.

Jack held up the envelope. "I'll be in touch soon."

The professor looked intently at Jack and made a slight bow. "Until then." He quickly gathered up his briefcase and left.

After the professor exited Punjeeh turned to Jack. "So how much did they offer you?" he asked.

Jack opened the envelope and scanned the document. He looked up and flashed his trademark grin. "One million dollars … U.S., of course."

Chloe let out a shriek. "That's great, Jack! Congratulations!"

"My god, man, you've always been lucky this way!" Punjeeh marveled.

Jack looked again at the offer. "I won't be accepting it," he said.

Punjeeh and Chloe were perplexed. "Now don't get greedy, Jack," Punjeeh warned.

"No, no … it's not that," he replied with a chuckle, "it's just that it's not my offer to accept. Professor King and I spoke earlier in the week, and we agreed that both of these scrolls belong to the two boys who found them. So the decision of whether to accept is up to them. I'm just acting as their agent in the process."

Punjeeh looked relieved. "With you in their corner, I have a feeling they will get the best deal available. And speaking of the boys, if we're going to visit them today we'd best get going. I'm sure they are anxious to hear from you."

Jack knew his old friend was right. The trouble was that his plane was leaving the next day and he wasn't sure when, or if, he'd see Chloe again. "Could I catch up with you in a minute, Punjh?" he asked, giving his friend the 'get the hell out of here' look.

Punjeeh took the hint. "Of course. I'll be in the car."

Jack turned to Chloe. "Yes, Jack, is everything okay?"

"Everything's great," he replied hesitantly. "I just wanted to thank you for everything, you've been a real help to me on the trip. I've learned a lot about history, religion, and maybe something about myself."

"It was my pleasure," Chloe assured him.

"And when you come to D.C., I would love to take you to dinner. I mean... I'm not trying to get in between you and Ben... if that is something serious."

Chloe was puzzled. "Ben?" she asked. "You mean my dog?"

Jack immediately turned bright red. "Ohhhh...," he said, "he's your dog. I misunderstood."

Chloe giggled. "And I would love to have dinner some time."

"Great!" Jack replied enthusiastically. "Because there are some other questions I want to ask you" – his tone turned more serious – "about the Bible."

Chloe was intrigued. "Oh... okay, and can you give me a hint as to what those might be?"

"It's about the Old Testament, since we really only talked about the New Testament, right?" he asked hesitantly, hoping he was getting the terminology correct.

"That's right, Jack," Chloe confirmed, "we barely mentioned the Old Testament."

"Good," Jack replied. "Because I'm curious: after everything I learned about Jesus and his miracles, do you think Moses really parted the Red Sea?"

*⌒⁄∕⌒*

# Epilogue

The red light began to flash on Chloe's telephone; she looked at the caller ID before picking up.

"Esther!"

"Sorry, Chloe, it's Punjeeh."

"Oh! Hi, Punjeeh!" she said.

"Is this a bad time?"

"No, I'm just sitting here at my desk, grading papers. What's up?"

"I've had a couple of days to think about the theories you put forward regarding the Gnostics, the crucifixion-resurrection, and the history of the early church, and now I have questions for you."

"I understand completely. Where would you like to begin?"

"St. Paul," Punjeeh answered quickly. "Let's talk more about St. Paul."

"Okay."

"His biblical letters are filled with references to Jesus' crucifixion. Isn't that a testimony to the fact that the crucifixion was a real historical event and not a story the Gnostics appropriated from the Mystery religions?"

"It's true that St. Paul's biblical letters frequently mention the crucifixion," Chloe answered, "but I would argue that it's actually his writings that provide some of the most compelling evidence that the crucifixion before Pilate *did not* take place."

"What?" Punjeeh asked incredulously, further puzzled by her response.

Consistent with her teaching style when in the classroom, Chloe preferred to begin every explanation from its most basic element, presupposing nothing. "Let's review what we know about St. Paul, so we're both on the same page, okay?"

"Agreed."

"Paul was born a Jew and lived during the first half of the first century CE. Although we don't know exactly when he was born, virtually all scholars agree he had reached adulthood by the time Pontius Pilate ruled Jerusalem. And it's clear from his biblical letters that he was well educated, spoke many languages, and traveled extensively throughout the Mediterranean world."

"That much I know," Punjeeh acknowledged.

"And you'd be surprised how many people make the mistake of believing Paul was one of Jesus' disciples—*he was not*. In fact, Paul never claims in any of his writings as to having ever known Jesus personally!"

"I knew that, too!"

"But despite the fact that he never met Jesus, Paul became Christianity's most successful advocate. His letters are some of the oldest Christian documents we have, written thirty to fifty years before any of the biblical gospels. Furthermore, he converted thousands of people to the fledgling religion by the mid-first century and is universally accepted by almost all Christian churches today as the most important person in Christianity, next to Jesus."

"So how do Paul's biblical letters support your claim about the crucifixion?" Punjeeh pressed.

"If you read Paul's letters carefully, you'll see that, as in the Gnostic gospels, the crucifixion has a very mystical and symbolic meaning for Paul. For if Jesus dying on the cross were a historical event, it is most remarkable that throughout the pages and pages of his biblical letters, Paul *never mentions* Pontius Pilate, Judas Iscariot, the garden at Gethsemane, Peter's denial of Jesus, the rock of Golgotha, or any of the facts associated with the crucifixion described in the biblical gospels! This is even more noteworthy when we remember that Paul was alive and well during the time these events were supposed to have taken place!"

Punjeeh was dumbstruck. "I've never noticed the absence of these things in his letters. How could I have missed this all these years?"

"Part of the reason is the order in which they appear in the New

Testament," she assured him. "Eusebius and the Literalist church placed Paul's letters after the gospels when they compiled the New Testament, even though they were written far earlier. This was not by accident. It gives the reader the impression that Paul is commenting on the events in the gospels, but modern scholarship suggests the opposite is true."

"Opposite?" Punjeeh asked, bewildered. "I'm not sure I'm following you."

"Besides the crucifixion, the only other specific act attributed to Jesus in Paul's letters is the communion ceremony. And, like the crucifixion, the communion ceremony is discussed by Paul in a highly symbolic way.

"Because Paul ascribed these two symbolic events to Jesus well before the gospels were written, many scholars argue that Paul did not learn about the crucifixion and communion ceremony from reading the gospels, but that the gospel writers learned about those events from reading Paul's letters."

"What?" Punjeeh cried.

"It's true! Many scholars now believe that the gospel writers took Paul's references to the communion ceremony and the crucifixion and then created the story of the Last Supper and Jesus' death at the hands of Pilate in order to provide Paul's teachings with a historical context."

"Unbelievable," Punjeeh said, shaking his head.

"And it's not surprising that the gospel writers chose Pilate as the villain," she continued. "His reputation for brutality was legendary, his favorite means of execution was crucifixion, and his persecution of the Jews was well documented by ancient historians."

"I guess it's not so different from many modern novelists," Punjeeh acknowledged, "who often place fictitious events in a historical time period to make them seem more real."

"And another interesting point along those lines," Chloe added, "is that Paul writes of meeting in Jerusalem with Peter, James, and John, whom he describes as leaders of the Jerusalem Christians. The Literalist church claims that these are the same Peter, James, and John who were the most prominent of Jesus' disciples in the gospels ... but it's important to point out that Paul never says that in any of his letters. In fact, he gives no mention of discussing the crucifixion with these men, which is really quite remarkable if they were witness to such an incredible historical event.

"Consequently, many scholars suggest that, as with the crucifixion and the communion ceremony, it's just as likely that the gospel writers took the names Peter, James, and John and assigned them to the most prominent of Jesus' disciples because they were mentioned as the Jerusalem Christian leaders in Paul's letters, not the other way around!"

"Amazing!" Punjeeh stammered. "And what about the other disciples then, the rest of the twelve?"

Chloe paused. "Do you still think there were actually twelve disciples? Many of the Mystery religion gods had twelve disciples too, as twelve was a very significant number in the religions of the ancient world. To the Greeks and Romans it represented the signs of the zodiac, the number of months in the lunar calendar. For the Jews converting to Christianity, the twelve disciples represented the twelve tribes of Israel. Jesus even hints at the representative nature of the disciples being twelve in number in the Gospel of Matthew, when he says, *'You who have followed me will sit on twelve thrones, judging the twelve tribes of Israel.'* Twelve would have been the logical choice for someone looking to synthesize Judaism with the Greek and Roman Mystery religions."

Punjeeh scratched his head. As usual, Chloe made a very convincing case for her theories, but he had promised himself prior to phoning that he wouldn't let her off easy. "Those are bold assertions, but they would be much weightier if you can prove Professor King's claim that Paul too was a Gnostic," he challenged. "What evidence is there of that?"

Chloe drew a breath. "They say you can tell a lot about someone by the friends they keep– so let's take a look at some of Paul's, shall we?

"First off, all the early Gnostic teachers, like Valentinus and Basilides, were so complimentary of Paul in their writings, often referring to him as 'the one true apostle.' Marcion, another highly influential Gnostic teacher who lived around 125 CE, claimed that it was only Paul's writings that contained the true essence of Christ's teachings. In short, it's clear that the earliest Gnostic teachers considered Paul one of them.

"Conversely, the Heresy Hunters and some other members of the early Literalist church were less than enthusiastic about Paul and his writings, even going so far as to try to discredit him. But ultimately Paul was too well known in the Christian community to ignore, as his letters were extremely popular with the faithful."

"I've read most of Paul's letters," Punjeeh added. "They're not what I would call light reading material."

"Yes, Paul's treatises are some of the most difficult and perplexing material in the Bible," Chloe confirmed. "In some parts they seem to flow with great ease and consistency; in others they are almost unintelligible... Scholars have concluded that he was either a horrible writer, a schizophrenic or, ... " she stopped in mid-sentence.

"Or what?" Punjeeh asked.

"That he wrote them that way on purpose."

Punjeeh ruffled his brow. "Why on earth would he do that?"

"The Gnostics claim Paul's letters were written in a type of secret code, and that he meant for his writings to be understood in two ways at once: one way by those who were spiritual, or the Gnostics, and another way by those who followed the letter of the law, the Literalists. Many scholars believe that the complexity of Paul's letters supports that he did intend them to have a dual meaning."

"Can you give an example?"

"If you remember," replied Chloe, "Paul often mentions in his letters that he is carrying Christ's message to two groups, the Jews and the non-Jews, those he called the Gentiles."

"Yes, yes," Punjeeh nodded, as his early religious training came back to him. "And the Roman Catholic Church often refers to Paul as the Apostle to the Gentiles, as the tone of his letters always seems to favor them."

"That's right. And if you examine Paul's writings carefully, you'll see that all his references to a strict observance of the law are aimed at the Jews, while the Gentiles were provided with more liberal, almost mystical guidance. The Literalist church took the words of Jews and Gentiles, well, literally. However, the Gnostics claimed that these references had nothing to do with ethnicity or culture, but instead, when Paul referenced the Jews, he really meant the Literalist members of the early church, and his references to the Gentiles were actually a coded way to address the Gnostics."

"Remarkable!"

"Combine all this with the fact that Paul grew up in Tarsus, a hot-bed for the Mystery religions. It's almost impossible to think that an educated, Greek-speaking, religious-minded person like Paul would not be aware of the communion and crucifixion-resurrection stories that abounded in the Mystery religions. On the contrary, he was well aware of the symbolism of stories like these, and that's why he mentions them repeatedly throughout his letters. As a Greek-speaking Jew who grew up in the Diaspora, he was a perfect candidate for synthesizing Judaism with the ideals of the Greek and Roman Mystery religions."

"That does make sense," Punjeeh conceded as he considered the implications of Chloe's arguments. "But in some ways this all sounds so strange, because I remember learning that Paul's biblical letters were anti-Gnostic."

"Two of Paul's letters are – those addressed to Timothy and Titus. But these two letters were not actually written by Paul, and they are the only ones that are anti-Gnostic."

"Wait a minute," Punjeeh said incredulously. "Are you saying that some of the letters attributed to Paul in the Bible are forgeries that weren't really written by him?"

"Without a doubt," Chloe shot back. "Even the most conservative scholars agree that these documents are fakes. They do not appear in the historical record until the time of the Heresy Hunters, or more than a hundred years after Paul's death, and it's clear these two let-ters were crafted with the intention of discrediting the Gnostics, and that they were included in the Bible for just that reason.

"In short, Paul's genuine letters give no historical or biographical information about Jesus, even though he is the one who is writing first after Jesus' death, before any of the biblical gospels."

"Amazing, simply amazing," Punjeeh replied, glancing at the notepad by the telephone. He had been careful to write down all his questions, so as not to forget anything. "I want to ask you more about the twelve disciples, which I know you already mentioned, but what about the biblical Acts of the Apostles? Doesn't this prove that these stories are historical accounts of real men?"

"Let's talk about the Acts of the Apostles," Chloe answered. "This New Testament book was originally claimed by the Literalist church to be a historical account of the travels and deeds of St. Paul and

Jesus' twelve disciples in the period immediately following Jesus' death. But here again, scholars have many reasons to doubt this interpretation of the facts."

"Why?"

"First off, we know that the Acts of the Apostles was written by the same person who wrote the Gospel of Luke. And while it's clear that the author of Luke copied extensively from the Gospel of Mark when writing Luke's gospel narrative, it appears as though he borrowed at least one story from the Greek poet Homer when writing the book of Acts!"

"*The* Homer?" Punjeeh asked incredulously. "The author of the *Iliad* and the *Odyssey*?"

"Yes, because, as you can imagine, very few people could read or write in ancient times. But for those who were literate, Homer's *Iliad* and *Odyssey* were the textbooks of the day. It's what the ancients learned to read by. Several ancient writers, even Plato, borrowed stories from Homer's works and transvalued them."

"What do you mean by transvalued?"

"Transvaluation is a literary technique that was popular in the ancient world. It's when an author takes a well-known story and changes the ending to give the story a new meaning."

Chloe tried to think of an example. "For instance, you're familiar with the children's story *Beauty and the Beast*, aren't you?"

"Yes."

"This classic tale has several versions in various cultures, but the ending is always the same: Upon falling in love with the hideous beast, Beauty transforms him back into a handsome prince with true love's kiss.

"Now, a transvaluation of that story would be that, after the climactic kiss, the beast maintains his grisly appearance. The point of the transvaluation would be to discredit the notion that true love is associated with outward beauty."

"Okay, I'm following you."

"Now, getting back to the Book of Acts and Homer," Chloe continued, "there was a well-known story from Homer's *Odyssey* about a young man named Elpenor, a traveling companion of Odysseus, Homer's main character in the work.

"Unfortunately for Elpenor, he met an untimely death one night when he fell from a rooftop after falling asleep. His story became an oft-quoted fable throughout the ancient world to explain unlucky events. For example, if fate seemed to conspire against you, someone might say, 'You're just like poor Elpenor,' and everyone would know that you had experienced an unlucky incident."

"That sounds like Murphy's Law," Punjeeh noted.

Chloe wasn't familiar with that American colloquialism.

"Murphy's Law states that if something can go wrong, it will," he explained. "When I went to college in the States, if something bad happened at an inopportune time, Jack would always say it was Murphy's Law."

"Yes, that sounds like a good example of what I mean," Chloe agreed. "And in the Acts of the Apostles, there is a story about a young man named Eutychus, a friend of St. Paul. In the biblical story, Eutychus also meets an untimely death one night when he falls from a building after falling asleep, just like Elpenor did in Homer's *Odyssey*.

"But here is where the story gets transvalued. In Homer's version, there was nothing Odysseus could do to save Elpenor after his death. His soul was condemned to Hades. But in the Book of Acts, when St. Paul learns of Eutychus' death, he performs the communion ceremony and then raises Eutychus from the dead ... so the message would have been clear to the ancients: Paul could do through the power of Jesus what Odysseus could not do through the gods of Ancient Greece."

Punjeeh continued to play the skeptic. "I'm not sure those stories are similar enough to say one was borrowed from the other."

"There's one more thing the author of Acts did to make sure the transvalued meaning was understood by ancient readers. Homer's story was so well known in ancient times that the name Elpenor came to mean *unlucky* ... but the name *Eutychus*? That's Greek, and it means '*the lucky one.*'"

Punjeeh threw up his hands. "I give up," he said good-naturedly.

"But don't let this negate the powerful messages contained in the book of Acts," Chloe added. "It's really quite a fascinating piece of work. In my opinion, its original purpose was to convey an important symbolic meaning, not to offer a record of historical events as the Literalist church later claimed."

"Symbolic?" Punjeeh's eyebrows went up. "How so?"

"If you examine the character of the disciples in the four bibli-cal gospels—that is, prior to their portrayal in Acts—you'll see that they are almost unequivocally presented as a band of bumbling buf-foons!"

Punjeeh couldn't help but chuckle at Chloe's statement.

"You may laugh, but it's true! Look at what the gospels tell us about the disciples: Peter denies Jesus, Thomas doubts him, and Ju-das is the betrayer, they argue amongst themselves as to which one of them is the greatest, the whole lot of them fall asleep in the garden of Gethsemane after Jesus asks them to stay awake, and, worst of all, throughout the entire Gospel of Mark they don't even realize Jesus is the Messiah!"

Punjeeh nodded his head. "Yes, in the biblical gospels the disciples are quite immature, if you will, for the roles they've been called to."

"But they are completely different people in the Book of Acts," Chloe countered. "Their characters have been 'reborn,' so to speak. They perform miracles, raise the dead, and are widely persecuted for their religious teachings. A careful reader will realize that the lives of the disciples in Acts mirror the life of Jesus in the gospels."

Chloe's last statement struck a chord with Punjeeh. "I've thought that exact same thing before, when I was a young boy, learning about the disciples. It occurred to me that after Jesus' crucifixion, they were completely different, it's as if they had been transformed."

Chloe liked Punjeeh's description. "Transformation is an excel-lent way to put it," she said. "And, not surprisingly, this transfor-mation was understood one way by the Literalists and another by the Gnostics. The Literalists attributed the change in the disciples' character as a direct result of a historical event: Christ dying on the cross for their sins. The Gnostics would view their transformation as a spiritual allegory, confirming that all of us can *become Christ-like* by experiencing gnosis."

Punjeeh shook his head. "Your explanations never cease to amaze me."

He then glanced at his notepad, being careful not to forget any-thing. "Let's go back to Jesus' crucifixion under Pilate. Didn't the Ro-man government have a record of that? I mean, this is one of the most celebrated events in human history!"

Chloe drew another breath. "That's another good point, as the Romans were very astute in the ways of governance, which included the practice of meticulous record-keeping. And that's why it's so amazing that in all the many surviving Roman documents from the first century, historians have never found any contemporary record, official or unofficial, that mentions the execution of a Jesus from Nazareth. Most Christians don't realize that the only recorded account of Jesus' crucifixion is in the biblical gospels themselves!"

"Amazing," Punjeeh muttered. "I thought surely an event like that would have been written down by some ancient historian."

"If it had happened like that, it probably would have! Instead, the oldest non-biblical reference to Jesus' crucifixion is a brief mention from the Jewish historian Josephus, writing in 93 CE, or more than sixty years after the events are alleged to have taken place. The Literalist church has always pointed to this as proof of Jesus' crucifixion, but one can easily see the problems with this argument, as writing some sixty years after an alleged event has taken place can hardly be considered a contemporary reference. It's just as likely that Josephus was repeating the Christian account of the crucifixion that had been in circulation for more than twenty years by that time, the one found in the Gospel of Mark.

"And another thing to remember," Chloe added, "is that, like all of Paul's letters, none of the Gnostic gospels found at Nag Hamadhi state that Jesus was crucified under Pontius Pilate either, which is undoubtedly the biggest reason why Eusebius and the Literalist church excluded these gospels from the canon of the New Testament when they assembled it more than three hundred years later."

"Amazing," Punjeeh added and scratched another question off his list. "One more thing, do you have any other evidence that Jesus and the Teacher of Righteousness were one and the same?"

Chloe grimaced. "That's a rather long answer," she replied and glanced at her wristwatch. "I don't mean to put you off, but to adequately address it would involve a more thorough discussion of the Essenes and the Dead Sea Scrolls than I have time for today. I have been asked to give a lecture on one of the Dead Sea Scrolls – the famed Copper Scroll of Qumran – at the Smithsonian Museum while I'm in Washington, D.C. Perhaps we can discuss this more after I complete my research for the lecture."

Punjeeh was reluctant to end the conversation. "If we must. And did you say a copper scroll?"

"Yes. It's quite an interesting anomaly. Unlike any of the other Dead Sea Scrolls, this treatise was engraved on copper instead of papyrus or leather. And what's even more intriguing is that it mentions a vast Jewish treasure that to this day has never been found."

"Unfound treasure?" Punjeeh marveled. "This is one topic I can't wait to hear more about."

# Selected Bibliography

Brooke, George J. *The Dead Sea Scrolls and the New Testament*. Fortress Press, 2005.

Doane, Thomas William. *Bible Myths and Their Parallels in Other Religions*. A comparison of the Old and New Testament myths and miracles with those of heathen nations of antiquity, considering also their origin and meaning. New York: C. P. Somerby, c1910.

Ehrman, Bart D. *Misquoting Jesus: The Story behind Who Changed the Bible and Why*, San Francisco: HarperCollins, 2005.

Ehrman, Bart D. *The New Testament: A Historical Introduction to the Early Christian Writings, Third Edition*. New York: Oxford University Press, 2004.

Ellegård, Alvar. *Jesus: One Hundred Years before Christ*. The Overlook Press, 2002.

Eusebius, Bishop of Caesarea. *Ecclesiastical History*. With an English translation by Kirsopp Lake. Cambridge, Mass.: Harvard University Press; London: W. Heinemann Ltd., 1926-1932.

Freke, Timothy, and Gandy, Peter. *The Jesus Mysteries: Was the "Original Jesus" a Pagan God?* Three Rivers Press, 2001.

Gibbon, Edward. *The Decline and Fall of the Roman Empire*. New York: The Modern Library, 1932.

Grant, Robert M. *Gnosticism and Early Christianity*. New York: Columbia University Press, 1966.

Harpur, Tom. *The Pagan Christ: Recovering the Lost Light*. Thomas Allen Publishers, 2004.

Helms, Randel. *Gospel Fictions*. Prometheus Books, 1988.

Inman, Thomas. *Ancient Pagan and Modern Christian Symbolism*. New York: Peter Eckler Publishing Company, 1922.

Irenaeus, Bishop of Lyons. *Against Heresies*. www.newadvent. org/fathers/0103.htm.

James, Edwin Oliver. *The Ancient Gods: The History and Diffusion of Religion in the Ancient Near East and the Eastern Mediterranean*. New York: Putnam, 1960.

Justin Martyr. *The First Apology*. www.newadvent.org/fathers/ 0126.htm.

Kingsland, William. *Gnosis or Ancient Wisdom in the Christian Scriptures or the Wisdom in a Mystery*. London: G. Allen & Unwin, Ltd., 1937.

Kuhn, Alvin Boyd. *Lost Light: An Interpretation of Ancient Scriptures*. Elizabeth, N. J.: Academy Press, 1940.

Lüdemann, Gerd. *Paul: The Founder of Christianity*. Prometheus Books, 2002.

MacDonald, Dennis Ronald. *The Homeric Epics and the Gospel of Mark*. New Haven, Conn.: Yale University Press, c2000.

Mack, Burton L. *Who Wrote the New Testament? The Making of the Christian Myth*. HarperSanFrancisco, 1989.

Pagels, Elaine. *Beyond Belief: The Secret Gospel of Thomas*. New York: Vintage Books, 2004, c2003.

Pagels, Elaine. *The Gnostic Gospels*. New York: Vintage Books, 1989, c1979.

Pagels, Elaine. *The Gnostic Paul*. Trinity Press International, 1992.

Pagels, Elaine. *The Origin of Satan*. New York: Random House, c1995.

Rhys, Jocelyn. *Shaken Creeds: The Virgin Birth Doctrine; a Study of Its Origin*. London: Watts & Co., 1922.

Robinson, James M. *The Nag Hammadi Library in English*. San Francisco: Harper & Row, 1990, c1988.

Wells, George Albert. *Did Jesus Exist?* London: Pemberton, 1986.

# Book Club Discussion Questions

**Spoiler Alert:** Hierophant Publishing has included the following questions to facilitate discussion for book clubs. Please note they are designed to be reviewed **AFTER** you have completed the novel.

1. What is the symbolism of the children's disagreement on the airplane? Other symbols to consider: Punjeeh's address, Sue Marino's room number, and Esther's choice of the *William Tell Overture*. Did you notice any other symbols not listed here?

2. Each of the four main characters (Jack, Punjeeh, Chloe, and Tariq) represents a different point on the spiritual path. How would you characterize each? Whom do you most identify with, if any?

3. Punjeeh frequently mentions beliefs and their impact on the human psyche. Describe your feelings about the power of belief. Do you agree with Punjeeh's point of view?

4. Were you surprised when Chloe announced that the crucifixion-resurrection story was borrowed from the Mystery religions? Keep in mind that she had already explained that the virgin birth and miracle stories were also borrowed. If you didn't expect the same of the crucifixion-resurrection story, why not?

5. How do you feel about the claim that the crucifixion-resurrection was an allegory, designed to symbolize the death of the lower self or ego? Does this explanation of the crucifixion-resurrection seem more believable than the traditional interpretation?

6. Do you share Chloe's opinion that even though the virgin birth, miracles, and crucifixion-resurrection stories are not historical facts, nothing changes about the main aspects of Jesus' teachings?

7. Imagine that you had never heard of the Christian religion and someone presented you with the accounts of Jesus' life in the biblical gospels of Matthew, Mark, Luke, and John. Would you be likely to view them as history or allegory?

8. Throughout the novel, Chloe and Professor King never use the word "pagan" to describe the Greek and Roman Mystery religions. Is "pagan" a loaded term? Had they used the word, especially early on, would it have affected your views on the believability of their claims?

# Order Form

*The Gnostic Mystery* is available for $14.95. Texas residents add 8.125% sales tax. Free shipping on 1-5 books. Please call for shipping rates on 5 or more books.

Name _____

Address _____

City, State, Zip _____

**Please send me \_\_\_\_\_ copies of:**

*The Gnostic Mystery* @ $14.95/copy $ _____

8.125% Sales Tax (TX residents) $ _____

Total Enclosed $ _____

**Make checks payable and mail to:**

Hierophant Publishing
8301 Broadway, Suite 219
San Antonio, TX 78209

Orders can be placed by phone with a credit card: (210) 829-0570 or online at www.hierophantpublishing.com

Credit card orders can also by faxed to (866) 553-9030.
Visa, MC, AMEX, and Discover.

Credit card # _____ Exp. date: \_\_\_ / _____

3 digit security code on back panel: _____

AMEX 4-digit security code: _____